SAHARA
Special

ESMÉ RAJI CODELL

HYPERION PAPERBACKS
FOR CHILDREN

NEW YORK

First Hyperion Paperback edition, 2004

1 3 5 7 9 10 8 6 4 2

Printed in the United States of America

The poem "Autobiographia Literaria" (pp. 111 and 174–175) is from *Collected Poems* by Frank O'Hara, copyright © 1971 by Maureen Granville-Smith, Administratrix of the Estate of Frank O'Hara. Used by permission of Alfred A. Knopf, a division of Random House.

This is a work of fiction. All names, characters, places, and incidents are either products of the author's imagination or used fictitiously. No reference to any real person is intended or should be inferred. Likeliness of any situations to any persons living or dead is purely coincidental.

Library of Congress Cataloging-in-Publication Data on file.

ISBN 0-7868-1611-2 (pbk. ed.)

Visit www.hyperionbooksforchildren.com

Love and thanks to Russell and Jim, ever patient and brilliant. A debt of gratitude to Julie Froman, Steven Malk, Sarah Packer, and Donna Bray, whose support and insight made this book happen.

To Beverly Cleary,
thanks

CONTENTS

CONTENTS

SAHARA
Special

1

Me and Darrell Sikes

Why did I write them? Love letters to nobody, nobody who loved me back. They made me feel foolish and better at the same time. I didn't know where to mail them, so I just saved the letters in my desk.

Dear Daddy,
How are you, I miss you, I love you,
I still love you, I'll always love you.

Sometimes I wrote, *When are you coming home?* Sometimes I wrote, *So you're never coming home, or are you coming home?* Sometimes I wrote, *You can come home now.* Sometimes I wrote, *Why didn't you take me with you?*

I didn't keep a very tidy desk.

One day the letters poured out over my lap,

my feet, my teacher's feet. I got some of the letters back, but most of them went to the counselor, Mr. Stinger. The worst part of being in his office was watching my mom read those letters. Her face looked gray, like my letters were bad news, death news. Was she thinking I loved her less because I missed my daddy more? I felt like I was floating on the ceiling, like smoke from something burning.

When I came down from the ceiling, I pouted. I wanted my letters back, all of them. I was so mad. Isn't there a law against reading other people's mail?

Mr. Stinger took out a stack of papers, a file full of the history of me. No, not *the* history. *A* history. A history that didn't include when me and my mom go to the bookstore. I can pick any book I want, even a book in hardcover. That's the way it's always been. We never have much money, but Mom doesn't blink when the numbers ring up. She hands over the big bills like she was buying milk or eggs, something we just can't do without. I love choosing books by the pile at the library, too, and listening to my mom read them to me, when she's not too tired from working. She has been my best teacher. But that's not in the history.

Mom looked at the file and her face went gray again, and again I felt gravity give out. Look at that, a pile of messy work, of unfinished work, a sloppy diary of me since Daddy left. Why didn't I write more carefully in third grade? Why didn't I finish that assignment in fourth grade? I watched as Mr. Stinger fed my letters back into the long file cabinet. The cabinet closed with a metal sound, a safe full of evidence against me. Waiting there for when they need to pull it out and call me dumb.

When we got out of the office, my mom talked in a low voice. "What do you want me to do, Sahara? Say I'm sorry that I couldn't keep him? Fine. I'm sorry. I *tried* my best. Can't a woman get a divorce without her kid going special ed on her?"

I wanted to say, *Don't be sorry, Mom, I couldn't keep Daddy either*, but I was wise now. I kept my mouth shut.

"You gonna let Daddy walk out with your

brain, too?" she grumbled. "Well, then, there's not going to be a vital organ left between us, is there! You just do your work, Sahara. They'll see they've made a mistake. You'll do it, won't you?"

I stared her in the eye, but I didn't answer her. I knew I was being fresh and bad, but I couldn't lie and say yes. Do it for what? Do it for who? They took what I gave them, they took what I didn't give them, they used it all the same way, to feed the file. I was through with giving them evidence. They wouldn't get anything more out of me.

Mom looked at me, furious. I thought she would slap me for the first time in my life. She didn't. She stomped away. I stood there, wishing she had slapped me. You're supposed to put an exclamation point at the end of strong feelings. A slap would have felt like that. But instead, her heels clicked out her punctuation, *dot dot dot.* . . .

I couldn't see where my sentence would end.

That file full of letters meant I met with a Special Needs teacher in the hallway to get something called Individualized Attention, and let me tell you, working in the hallway with a teacher is like being the street person of a school. People pass you by, and they act like they don't see you, but three steps away they've got a whole story in their heads about why you're out there instead of in the nice cozy classroom where you belong. Stupid? Unlucky? Unloved? If I could have put out a cup, I would have made some change. People from my class would hiss, "Hi, Sahara Special" as they passed to go to the washroom, and don't think they meant special like a princess or a movie star or something sparkly like that. I pretended like I didn't hear, but oh yes, I heard, and you don't just hear meanness with your ears. My cheeks heard it and turned red, my eyes heard it and stared at the wall, at my lap, at my shoes. My fingernails heard it, and hid away in my teeth. I heard it all through my clothes and skin and blood and all the way to my bones, where it rattled in the hollow of me.

The Special Needs teacher told me her name when I met her, but I forgot it right away. Seeing her day after day, I was too embarrassed to ask what it was. In my mind, I just called her Peaches. In the real world, I didn't call her anything at all. In the hallway Peaches played board games with me and talked in a whispery, cooing voice like I was a doll and we were having a pretend tea party. I ignored her as best I could to keep from throwing up on her. She would sometimes ask me if I had done my homework and I would pretend I didn't hear. She spoke about using time well, getting things done. "Don't you agree that would make life a lot easier?"

I'd nod; sure, I'll agree to that. In fact, I thought, if I were *really* the school street person, I could *drink* to that, toast to it using the white milk in a carton they give at lunch, only keeping it in a brown paper bag. *Herrrre'sssss to the people who usssse timmmme well and get thinnnngsssss donnnnne!*

I couldn't help but laugh.

"What's so funny?"

I'd just shrug. She probably wouldn't think it was funny. I'd never seen her laugh. She'd write something down. Probably: *Laughs for no reason. Finds organization funny.*

Peaches seemed very organized. I bet nothing fell out of her desk in her whole life.

Then she'd ask if there was anything I wanted to talk about, and when I would say no, she would smile sweetly and look unhappy at the same time.

Sometimes Darrell Sikes would sit with us in the hall. I think he has been Special Needs ever since dinosaurs roamed the earth, or at least since the Declaration of Independence was signed. He kicked a teacher in the shins when he was in first grade, and when he was in third grade he was finally tall enough to punch one in the nose. At least, that's what people *say*, but who knows what's true? Mom says not to judge a book by its cover. Even so, I couldn't help but think that if Darrell was a book, the cover would read *True Crime Stories*. Darrell never spoke one word to me, and wouldn't look at me, and I thought he was a real gentleman for it. I did the same for him.

Darrell had a different set of manners for Peaches. Darrell grunted at her as if anytime she asked him something she was disturbing him from a nap. If we were playing a board game, he would roll the dice and move his piece backward. If Peaches asked him a question, he would answer by asking, "Are you married?" and batting his eyes, looking very interested. Sometimes he would smash everything off the table with a clatter, and swear.

"I'm afraid I am going to have to call your mother," Peaches said calmly.

"Well, don't you be *afraid*! You just go ahead and call her!" Darrell hollered. "You think she care? If she care, why the hell would I be out here in the hall with *you*?"

I told my mom about this, and all about oh how *funny* Darrell is, and the next day she came to the school and we had another meeting with Mr. Stinger and Peaches. "I want her out of the program," she said, "or whatever it is you've got going on here. I'm not sending her to school to sit in the hallway with some lunatic."

"He's not some lunatic," corrected Mr. Stinger. "He's a human being with special needs."

"Special needs!" my mom sputtered. "The only special need that boy has is for an old-fashioned crack across his behind! My daughter isn't spending part of her day with a teacher beater."

"It's just what people *say*, Mom." I pulled on her sleeve. "Don't judge a book—" She shook me off.

"Your daughter needs support during this time," Mr. Stinger reminded her, and Peaches nodded. I thought to myself, that teacher just wants someone to play Uno with.

"Maybe we should ask *Sahara* what she wants," Peaches suggested, with her usual sad-happy smile.

"Is this Christmas? Are you the Special Needs Santa Claus? Ask Sahara what she wants!" Mom twisted in her seat and made a noise between a cough and a laugh. "Look, I don't have time for this. I know she's capable of fifth-grade work. She reads at home. She reads plenty. I think she writes, too," she said accusingly. I didn't look at her. She whirled around in her chair and growled at me, "Sahara, tell them you like to write."

She was telling it true. I read at home, and write, too, but whatever I write, I make sure I'm by myself and then, when I'm done writing, I rip it out of my notebook. I hide it in a binder behind section 940 in the public library, where all the books about Somewhere Else are located. This very paper, for instance, will someday be an archaeological find. Someday, someone will reach behind section 940 and find the dusty works of me, Sahara Jones, Secret Writer, and that person's life will be made more exciting, just by reading my *Heart-Wrenching Life Story and Amazing Adventures*. Someday, people will be glad I kept track. Someday, people will see I am a writer. And because I am writing a true story of my life I have to talk about school, since I am still a kid and it is a very big part of my *Heart-Wrenching Life Story and Amazing Adventures*. I am sorry to report that school is heavy on the Heart-Wrenching but so far has been running low-to-empty on Amazing Adventures. But I still go, because maybe one day I will have an Amazing Adventure there. Also, both the law and my mother make me go, unless I am sick with chicken pox or getting a tooth pulled or going to a funeral. So school is a lesser evil. Usually.

"Yes, I like to write," I squeaked.

Mom bounced her purse on her lap and smiled as if to say, "So there."

Mr. Stinger looked at me sideways for a moment. "Yes. The letters."

No, *not just the letters*, I wanted to tell him. *Not just those stupid stupid stupid stupid stupid stupid letters that grew legs to follow me around.* "So, can I have those letters back now?" I tried to sound like honey with sugar on top.

"Well, we need something to show that you like to write, don't we, Sahara?" Mr. Stinger smiled. "We certainly don't have any schoolwork to make that point. And this is what I'm talking about. Where is the work, Mrs. Jones? *Where is the work?* She doesn't do it here."

"You're saying she doesn't do her work? So take care of your business! Fail her! Fail her like a normal kid. The failure will be between me and my daughter, then. You won't like it if her failure is between me and you."

"There are serious repercussions to retention. . . ."

"Blah blah blah!" My mother can be very rude.

So they promised to fail me. "Remember, you asked for it," they said to my mother. They made her sign a form. Then another. Then another.

The door closed, and we stood out in the hall. I knew they were talking about my mom behind the glass, saying mean things about her, about What Sort of Mother Would Deny Her Child Individualized Attention. But Mom was smiling and I was proud, really proud of my mom not being afraid of failure. I am. I'd sooner not try than fail. They may think I'm stupid, but I'm not. Knowing I'm not stupid is enough for me, I'm enough for me. When my mother smiled at me, I could see I was enough for her, too. At least, for that moment.

I walked back to my classroom, past the little table outside the door where Darrell was sitting in the public of the hallway waiting for Peaches to return, drawing on the side of his shoe with a black marker. He didn't look at me and I didn't look at him. But in my head, I said, *Oh, thank you, Darrell Sikes, for being wild and nasty and rude and getting me out of The Program and making me*

Normal Dumb, not Special Dumb. I owe you one, Darrell Sikes.

But I could not imagine how I would ever pay him back.

2

My True Ambition

I like when my mom listens to me in the kitchen, when she asks me about my day. She always asks if there's anyone new I'm hanging out with or if I'd like to bring anyone by the restaurant. She asks even though my best friend stays the same: my very own cousin, Rachel Wells.

Rachel is a year younger than I am. Rachel's voice is like pages turning, whispery and smooth, and there's time in between each thing she says. She looks at her feet when she speaks in her paper voice, and her cheekbones get pink like she's telling you about the time she forgot to wear her underwear even if she's just telling you what she had for dinner last night. Rachel moved away for a while with her mother, father, and little baby brother, Freddie. She came back with her mother and brother. My mom and her mom find a lot to talk about together. Rachel left the same time my father left. But Rachel came back.

That is reason number one she is my best friend.

Some of the girls at school thought Rachel was stuck-up, but I knew she wasn't. For real, shy girls usually aren't. They usually care more than anyone else about what other people think. It's like they're walking on ice, and the ice is made of other people's opinions. But there's something not-nice about shy people, too. Something kind of stingy in the way they make you talk first, and then their answers are just one word. That's why it took so long for Rachel to join us upper graders in double Dutch. Always holding back. I had to go over to the fence, special, to get her.

"Rachel, oh come on, take your turn, jump, jump!"

But she wouldn't, not for the longest time. Even now, she always lets other people jump first while she turns the ropes. So reason number two that she is my best friend is because I always have to look out for her.

And reason number three is the fact that she's the only one who knows my True Ambition.

But for now, nobody can see my True Ambition, so nobody believes it. I only believe it because I saw it, just once, just for a second. I saw it in a crystal ball. All right, it wasn't a crystal ball, it was a goldfish bowl turned upside down. It was the middle of summer, and Rachel and I needed something to do, so we tried telling fortunes at the kitchen table.

"What do you see?" I asked Rachel.

"Nothing," she shrugged.

I waited for her to ask me the question back, which is the polite thing to do. I got tired of waiting.

"Know what I see?"

"What?"

"Nothing," I said, just to be mean. But I did see something. I saw my own reflection, turned upside down. Something in me tilted, and I knew. "No, wait, I see something," I announced to Rachel. "I'm going to be a writer." The words came out all by themselves.

"*You?*" She blew some air through her nose and shook her head.

"What?"

"Like, a *writer* writer? With a *book*? In the *library* or something?"

It sounded so good! "Uh-huh."

"What are you going to write about?"

"Oh, just . . . stuff."

"What stuff?"

What stuff? "Everyday stuff. Interesting stuff."

She looked at me like I was homework. "Everyday stuff isn't interesting stuff," she pointed out. She took out a deck of cards from the kitchen drawer and began to shuffle them. "Writing a book's too hard."

"How would you know? You've never even tried."

"I never tried 'cause it's too hard. I wouldn't write a book unless somebody made me. I have no *in-ter-est*," she explained.

"Well, I'm going to make me," I announced. "I have interest. I am going to be the youngest writer ever to have a book in the library. You'll see."

Rachel looked at me hard, like she saw the sparkling of Lake Michigan in my eyes. I smiled at her, and hoped she saw good things, exciting things. She blinked, and frowned. No, she just saw my eyes, brown. Brown like brick, like the high-rises that block my view east, block my view of the lake, block my view of what's moving with hardness and stillness and curtains hung crooked. The buildings hunker there, like boxes in a closet, blocking the way to hidden birthday gifts or other surprises the grown-ups haven't told us about. But I know exciting things are there, hidden, just a matter of pushing past.

"Then you better get a good teacher this year, Sahara," Rachel warned, like I have anything to do with *that*. Why does she have to talk to me like she's grown?

"I need *support*, huh." I flashed her a look. Rachel must have decided there were no more fortunes to tell, because, back and forth, she dealt the deck for War. She turned over an ace of spades. "Jeez, Rachel. Don't you ever make any wishes?"

"Well . . . I would like to be able to see without glasses. And to not have to watch Freddie so much. And . . . I guess I wouldn't mind having a cousin who's a famous writer," she said, collecting my two of hearts.

I bring home a big pile of books to read every week. I usually stay inside, because we do not live in a good neighborhood. When my mom sends me to the corner store, she watches for me out the window the whole time, and I see Mrs. Rosen watching, too. She is so old and shrunken, her head is hardly higher than her window box, but there is her head, like one of the flowers. I don't like the men sitting in the cars and drinking on the street, or the low-riders that pass with the bass so loud on the radio that my fillings rattle. Rachel and I are allowed to skate up and down the block, but in the summer Rachel usually goes to Cordelia Carbuncle's house to play in their yard, and I am not invited. I tell myself it is because I am older. I

tell myself I am glad. I don't even like Cordelia.
Rachel has lost her glasses three times on purpose,
because Cordelia told her there is not one single
famous model who wears glasses. So when I went
to the dentist I borrowed a copy of *Seventeen* from
the waiting room and drew glasses on all the girls.
It made Rachel laugh, but she still tries to copy
Cordelia and does what she says. For instance,
Cordelia's momma lets her wear makeup. Rachel
complained so much that her momma let her wear
lip gloss on Sundays. It did look kind of pretty, so
I asked my mom if I could wear makeup on
Sundays, too.

"The only reason a girl your age should wear
makeup is if she's a rock star or a hooker, and the
minute you start showing promise in either of those
areas we'll hop on down to Target and stock you up
with everything you need," she promised. "Don't you
tell your auntie I said that, now. What she does with
Rachel is her business. I just happen to think there
is nothing more attractive than a sensible girl," she
said.

"To who?"

"To *who*? To *God*," she said. "And when you go to God's house, it ain't got to be no fashion show. You just come as you are." She gave me a squeeze. I think if my mom had to name her best friend, I might top the list.

But Cordelia tops Rachel's list. Rachel and Cordelia like to sit out front when she comes to visit. When the teenage boys say hi to Cordelia, she says hi back. Rachel doesn't exactly say hi, but she acts busy with her baby brother on her lap or smiles that terrible well-I-don't-know-what-else-to-do smile that makes me cluck my tongue and want to pinch her.

"How come you don't say hi?" Cordelia asked me once.

"I don't know them."

"They're just being friendly."

"They've got no business being friendly."

"That's why you don't have any friends," said Cordelia in a perky way.

"I do too have friends."

"Yeah? Who?"

"Beezus. Beezus Quimby."

21

"That's a *peculiar* name," said Cordelia.

"So's *Carbuncle*," I said. "Maybe if you didn't make fun of people's names, *you'd* have more friends. Come on, Rachel, let's go upstairs."

On the stairwell, I talked low. "Don't talk to strange men, Rachel. We don't have daddies to beat them up if they come bother us."

Rachel nodded and asked me, "Who's Beezus?"

"I met her when you moved away," I said, "and then she moved when you came back to town."

Rachel does not like to read. She likes to watch TV. So does Freddie. He bounces in his playpen when the people on the talk shows start throwing punches. Sometimes I am in her apartment, but mostly I stay in mine, which mom says is fine as long as I lock the door if she's at work. I open all the windows and the breeze and music from the ice-cream man floats through and lifts the curtains. I lie on my bed with my feet up on the wall and read. I roller-skate around the apartment until Mr. Martinez knocks his broom on the ceiling. I write in my notebook and rip out the pages to take to the library. I make lunch of canned sweet corn and boiled hot dogs, which I pierce with a fork and hold over the gas burner to turn the skin black, just like a real campfire, just like my daddy taught me. My daddy was a great cook. He even did it for a while for a living. My daddy could do anything. He liked to try new things.

New things all the time.

3

At the Library

$\mathcal{M}$om tries to get the Saturday morning shifts at the restaurant. The tips are good, and I love it because she drops me off at the library. I can stay until noon, and then she runs and gets me and brings me back to the restaurant, and I can have pancakes. The library is so air-conditioned that I have to bring a sweater, and when I go in I just have to say "Ahhhh," it feels so cool. I sit near the librarians, like sitting near the bus driver on the bus, it's just safer. They smile and say hello, but they don't talk to me, which doesn't feel as mean as it sounds. It just feels calm and ordinary. I sit in a big brown straight-back chair at a big brown table of smooth wood. I like to sit there and write my life story or read the Ramona books by Beverly Cleary. When I read those books, the rest of the world melts away and I am on Klikitat Street. Ramona has a dad, and sometimes the mom and dad have fights. But they never break up. Sometimes I read the books twice, but the endings never change. In a story, if you write a happy ending, it never has to change. It stays happily ever after.

Sometimes the books have pictures of the authors on the inside back covers. It's fun to see what they look like. Sometimes they look much older than I thought they would be, or are a different color than I imagined. Sometimes there isn't any picture of them at all, just a description of how they live in Massachusetts with two dogs or something. But real, live authors wrote every one of those books, so the shelves are like lines of quiet people, sitting up straight and polite, waiting to talk to me. Someday I'll have a book of my own. Someday my book will talk.

The library has regulars on Saturdays, mostly mothers with babies and toddlers, but there is one girl I notice who is close to my age. She usually wears pigtails, but her hair is so kinky that they look round and funny, like mouse ears. She has a nick, some kind of scar in the hair of her left eyebrow that makes her look serious even when she is smiling. She is skinny and always comes with her skinny brothers, all older than her, who swarm around her but don't seem to bother her as she picks out books. She mostly goes to the arts-and-crafts section, but sometimes she pokes around *my* section, with all the books about faraway places. I have to watch her then, because I am worried and excited that she might discover that my papers are hidden there, but she doesn't. She just pulls out the books and reads them cross-legged on the floor. She puts a pencil in the spot where she takes out a book so she can put it back in the same place. She's very organized.

Once I was watching her and she looked up at me, straight into my face. I almost died. But her eyes were steady.

"Hi," she said.

I waved, even though she was right in front of me.

"You look familiar," she said, and pulled her lip, trying to remember where she might have seen me before. *Probably sitting out in the hallway at school*, I thought. I felt my cheeks get warm, and I couldn't decide what to say or where to make my eyes go. She shrugged, and seemed to give up trying to figure it out. "You're here regular, huh?" she said.

"Yeah," I said.

"Me, too." She smiled. "My mother makes my brothers take me. She hopes they'll look at some books, but they never do. They just wait for me and drive the librarians crazy." She let out a little laugh, and I joined her. "I'm Paris," she said.

"The city?"

"No. The girl." She looked in the direction of her brothers, who seemed to give her some secret signal. "Well, see ya," she said all of a sudden, and jumped up to join them.

I couldn't stop thinking about Paris and imagining talking to her. *My name is Sahara. The girl, not the desert. Oh, do you like to read? So do I. What do you like to read? So do I. I like your hair. How do you get it*

*to do like that? Sure, I would love to come over. Let me
ask my mom. . . .*

"Who you talking to?" Mom calls from the
kitchen. I did not notice I had said anything out
loud.

"Nobody," I answer. I rehearse some more, but
I am careful to keep it inside my head. I imagine
bringing Paris to the restaurant where my mom
waitresses. I imagine sitting on the high stools at
the counter with her. *Look what a big pile of pancakes! Oh, Sahara!* I imagine my mom's face as she
heads back to the kitchen, after putting down
plates for me and my best friend. The thought of it
makes my insides bubble.

The next Saturday, though, Paris brought just
one brother and a girl, a Spanish-looking girl with
long black hair and glittery butterflies on her
shirt. They leaned over a cookbook together, at the
big table. *Let's make this. Let's make this.* I sat apart
from them, behind them. As they left, Paris
noticed me in my corner. "Oh, hi!" she said. "I was
looking for you! I didn't see you."

Really? "Hi," I said.

"Didn't you see *me*?" she asked.

The question took me by surprise. "No," I lied. She looked at me, holding her cookbooks against her chest, as if trying to decide something. I looked away from her and pretended to go back to reading. *Who cares about you?* I thought. *Go bake your brownies.*

But she didn't leave right away. She seemed to stand there staring at me for a long time. Her friend waited patiently in the doorway. What were they waiting for?

"Wellll . . . bye," she said finally.

She left. "Well, bye," I said.

I sat for a long time and counted the books in a pile in front of me. I counted them up and I counted them down. But just then I didn't feel like reading any.

4

New Things All the Time

"You nervous about school?" Mom asked the evening before school started. She was washing potatoes at the sink as I packed a peanut-butter sandwich at the table.

"No, it's going to be fine," I said, thinking of being in the same class with Rachel and no more Special Needs in the hallway.

"You do, huh. Well, I hope so." Mom gave me a poison eyeball. I guess she was not thinking about my being with Rachel and no more Special Needs in the hallway. I slowly folded the foil around my sandwich and slid it into my backpack.

"All those books you read," she went on, not even looking at me while she peeled potatoes in short, fierce strokes. She was smacking them with

the peeler like she wished they were my bottom.
"What a waste, Sahara, what a waste. Talk about a
crying shame, Sahara, it's just a crying shame, you
read all the time and what for? Repeating fifth
grade! How can such a smart . . . ! Tsk! Huh! I just
don't understand you." She turned around suddenly and faced me, her chin jutting out and
moving back and forth, but no words came then.
She turned back to the sink. *Peel. Peel. Peel.* Trying
to find me somewhere under the skin, the daughter she could be proud of. I just ran my finger over
the smooth finish of my folders. I'm getting better
at keeping things tidy, I told myself.

"I'm going for a walk," I surprised myself by
saying.

"Oh, no you're not," said Mom. "Where you
think you're walking to?"

"It's still light out," I said. I walked out before
she could say anything and ran down the stairs,
even though I could hear her through the door,
calling me.

I walked toward the corner store, but once I
hit the corner, where was I supposed to go? I still

turned it, because I knew my mother was watching me through the window, and I was mad at her.

But once I was out of her sight I didn't walk anymore. I just sat on somebody else's stoop and put my head on my knees and cried.

My mom was there in a minute. She walked me back, holding my shoulders.

She sighed. "Let's just take it a day at a time, okay, Sahara?"

But I'm too lonely, I wanted to tell her. *I can't do it.*

But the sun rose again, on the first day of fifth grade for a second time. It rose and said, You're going to have to do it.

As I was walking in, no teacher was there, and the door was open. I took a seat in the back of the room, like always. Rachel chose a seat in the row in front of me, to my left. She turned and smiled apologetically. I smiled back. No hard feelings; the back row's not for everybody. She motioned to the seat in front of the one I'd chosen, but I pretended to be busy organizing my folders. I couldn't explain to Rachel that the seat in front of me was reserved, hopefully for someone very tall and easy to hide behind.

I looked at my new classmates. I knew a few of the girls from double Dutch: there was Sakiah and Tanaeja, and I knew Kiarre by sight, she's so tall and tough. I knew a couple of the boys: big-mouthed Raphael, Ernie who comes to the library sometimes, and Darrell, held back like me, legs spread, frowning in the back-row corner. Was that handsome boy's name Dominique? There was Paris on the other side of the room, and the girl with the black hair, too, chatting away. Paris waved, and I waved back. They seemed nicer than my old class, maybe because Cordelia hadn't made it back in time from her family vacation to Disney World, maybe because it was the first day, and everyone was clean, everyone was on good behavior. I looked at Darrell. *Better* behavior. The class was smaller than most. I noticed that this was usually the case when Darrell was in the roll. *Maybe I'll have new friends*, I thought fleetingly, but my mind was not really on my classmates. There was someone left I needed to meet.

The vice-principal was standing there. "Are you our new teacher?" someone asked.

"No." He looked relieved. "The fifth-grade teacher moved on over the summer," he said.

"She quit!" a voice called out.

The vice-principal frowned, but he couldn't tell who said it, so he ignored it. "Yes, well! Your new teacher is on her way."

"Is she a teacher from another class?" someone asked. Our minds raced. The patient kindergarten teacher, wagging a puppet on each hand? The short-tempered seventh-grade teacher with hair growing from his ears, the one who likes to be called "Lieutenant"? I shivered.

"It's no one you know," the vice-principal explained. "She'll be transferring in from some-where else. Be seated. Someone will be with you shortly." He excused himself.

A teacher from Somewhere Else sounded good to me. Sometimes, I wish I were from Somewhere Else myself. I wish I were from the sort of place that inspires you to write long sentences about the shapes of clouds and the smell of things growing. But when you're from Chicago, it's hard to write sentences that sound like anything except coins going into the change machine on the public bus. *Clink. Clank. Clunk.*

Clunk.

"Teacher's coming!" hissed a boy who was standing guard at the door of the classroom. "I think this is her!" He slid into his chair.

"Is she ugly?" asked another boy.

"Shhh! She'll hear, fool," snarled a girl. "Momma says, 'You never get a second chance to make a first impression.'" She folded her hands and smiled at the ceiling.

I closed my eyes and tried to enjoy the feeling of the teacher not knowing me yet. I think I could do my work here. It's been a while. But what's the use? Even if this teacher I'm dealt is a queen of diamonds, I don't want to give them any more material for their file about me. Their precious file, so different from my own file of my summer, tucked behind books in the low shelf of the library. I try to put this file out of my head and sit up straight.

And that's when I notice it is so quiet we can hear her coming down the hall. We are not even blinking, frozen like statues in our first-impression poses.

What's in *her* file, I wonder? And then I can't help snickering a little, even though it breaks my pose.

Because if they kept files on grown-ups, it would be a different story, wouldn't it?

5

We Got Her

*I*n she walked. Our new teacher!

I blinked, and blinked again. Her hair was copper like a lucky penny, but when the light hit it a certain way, it seemed almost green, a deep green, like she colored it with a dye made from tree leaves. It was held back with sparkling dragonfly barrettes, but there was no help for it. It was wild hair. She was pale, but I couldn't decide for sure if she was white or Asian or Puerto Rican, or maybe light-skinned black. When someone is wearing lipstick as purple as an eggplant, it's hard to tell. She wore lime eye shadow and heavy black liquid eyeliner, making her expression catlike. She wore a yellow dress that looked like it was made of tissue paper, kind of old-fashioned and grandmotherly, but hanging slightly over her shoulder. Her bra strap was showing. It was also purple. She looked less like a teacher and more like one of those burnt-out punk-rocker teenagers who hang out in front of the Dunkin' Donuts on Belmont, near the L stop. Only grown.

Her arms were full of flowers. She opened up her desk drawer and pulled out a scissors, and sat down, cutting each stem at an angle. Then she swiveled in her chair and pulled out a vase from a cabinet behind her, and arranged the flowers. We all watched, caught up in where she moved the daisies and sunflowers, tilting our head along with her, this way, then that way. "Ever been to a farmers' market?" she asked the air, her eyes still on the flowers. "The flowers there aren't like the ones at the grocery store, oh no, it's a whole different deal. Imagine, these beauties, for sale in the middle of a parking lot! I swear, you can get anything your heart desires in the city, I don't see why *anyone* ever settles for *less*." She swiveled again, and pulled out a watering can. "Please." She thrust it at a girl in the first row. We all jumped—it was the first time she seemed to notice that any of us were there, and we had all forgotten where we were, too.

The girl left the room to fill the can. In the meantime, the woman sized up the space on the wall behind her desk. Then she whipped out a hammer, and a nail went into the wall with a brisk *bang, bang, bang*. We jumped again. She hung a framed diploma on it. If I narrowed my eyes, I could see it said MRS. FRUMPER'S FABULOUS SCHOOL FOR TEACHERS in fancy handwriting. She straightened it carefully, put her hand over her heart and blew through her lips in a satisfied way. Then she pulled out a table lamp with a shade of thin red glass, shaped like a tulip. Six clear crystals hanging all around the base of the shade shimmered and sang like small bells when they moved against each other. She unhooked each crystal and polished it with a handkerchief she pulled out from whatever it was she was wearing under her clothes. She held each crystal up to the light in turn, and squinted. We all squinted.

A boy raised his hand.

The teacher glanced at the clock on the wall, five minutes until nine, then back at the boy.

"Do you have to go to the washroom?"

"No."

"Then put your hand down," she said, hard and quick, like the hammer banging. The boy obeyed.

She hung the last polished crystal, and turned the little lamp on and off, to test it. "Working lights are important things," she remarked, again, to the air. "A light that won't go on, well, that's just sad."

The girl returned with the watering can. The woman filled the vase and pushed it forward on her desk. She felt for her pearls and adjusted them, making sure the clasp was at the nape of her neck. Then she sat, her lips against her fist, and looked us over one by one, with the concern of a dentist peeking into a very wide and decaying mouth.

The bell rang.

The teacher sighed and got up, moving around to the front of her desk and leaning against it, her arms crossed. She looked like she might be smiling, but the smile was tucked away like a mint against her gum and cheek. "Well," she said. "Another year.

"My name is Madame Poitier, Miss PWAH-tee-YAY. It rhymes with *touché*, a French word that means, 'you got me.'" She smiled openly then, even though it was the first day of school. I had never seen a teacher do that before.

"Most children call me Miss Pointy," she continued. We giggled. "Some children just call me Madame."

"My damn what?" Darrell called out.

"Your damn teacher," Miss Pointy replied without blinking, "and this seems like a perfect moment to talk about rules. What do you think some good rules would be?"

Kids called out. No talking. No pushing. No chewing gum. No taking other people's stuff. No swearing. No not doing homework. No pulling hair. No chair-kicking. No copying. No calling names.

Miss Pointy yawned. "How about, No rules that start with the word *no*? Haven't you kids ever heard the word *yes*?" She wrote on the board:

YES looking

YES listening

YES consideration

"What's consi . . . consid . . ."

"Consideration? Treating other people the way you want to be treated. If you don't like being pushed, or having your stuff taken, or having your hair pulled, don't do it, or you may be paid back in the same coin. That's common sense. YES common sense. And YES, hard work, harder than you've ever worked in your whole lives, so if you want extra credit, get a head start on sweating. I'm the meanest teacher in the west."

"Do you shoot from the hip?" snickered Raphael.

"You'll find out, cowboy." Miss Pointy's nostrils flared.

She wrote the schedule on the board.

Puzzling, 9:10 to 10:40
Time Travel and World Exploring or

Mad Science,
alternate days, 10:40 to 11:30
Read Aloud, after lunch
Read Together after Read Aloud,
Read Alone after Read Together
Art of Language, end of the day

What did it all mean? We looked at each other. None of us knew, none of us asked. We were all feeling too shy, except for Darrell, who maybe didn't care.

Miss Pointy passed out thick composition books with black-and-white marbled covers. "You each owe me two dollars," she announced as she passed them out.

"I don't got two dollars," complained a boy.

"You may not *have* two dollars now, but some-day you will. Then you'll pay me."

She continued to pass out the books, and one skidded across my desk. I stopped it with my hand, and smiled. It was nice to get something new.

"This is your journal," she explained. "You will

write in it every day. Begin each entry with the date. 'Dear Diary' or 'Dear Journal' is *optional*, or up to you. I'll read and sometimes comment on what you write, unless you make a 'P' with a circle and a line through it on the top of the page, like this." She drew on the board.

"This means, 'None of your business, Miss Pointy.' What you write is between you and the paper, and sometimes me," she promised.

"And the Special Needs teacher," Darrell grumbled.

"I don't like bureaucrats," she told Darrell, "but I don't mind cynics."

"What's a bureaucrat?" Darrell asked suspiciously.

"A tattletale who likes to write things down," Miss Pointy explained.

"Oh, like Sakiah," a girl called out.

"I don't know that Sakiah tells on people yet," said Miss Pointy. "So far, I only know that about *you*." The girl turned red; Miss Pointy winked, forgiving.

"She does shoot from the hip!" Raphael howled. We laughed some more.

"What's a cynic?" asked Paris.

"Someone who sees the world through mud-colored glasses. Mud's easy enough to clean up, though. 'God made dirt and dirt don't hurt', that's what my little brother used to say. Right before he ate dirt."

We looked at Miss Pointy and couldn't help smiling. A teacher who had a brother who ate dirt! A teacher who would lend you two dollars! A teacher who was going to show us how to travel through time and to solve puzzles! So, she used big words and shot from the hip. Those two things could be overcome. All other signs pointed to human.

"Now. Line up against the wall. I'm picking your seats. No whining. Come on, come on. Now. You—there. You—there. You—there; no—there." I was relieved when I was seated in the back of the room again. When all of us were seated, she scrutinized the arrangement. "You," she pointed.

"Who, me?"

"Change places with her."

Second row. Rachel and I passed each other. How did Miss Pointy know I was . . . well . . . hiding? "And you," she pointed to Darrell Sikes. "Up here, too."

"Why I gotta sit in the front row!"

"All the better to see you, my dear," said Miss Pointy.

"Dang!" Darrell got up as slowly as if he weighed eight hundred pounds and sauntered forward. He finally slammed his book bag and body into place with such force, he could have been crash-landing off the top of a skyscraper.

"Oh, a thespian." Miss Pointy sniffed. "Your stage business is sluggish. We'll have to work on your pacing."

"What's a thespian?" asked Tanaeja.

"An actor."

"I ain't no actor!" Darrell exploded. "I'm Darrell Sikes, and you better watch your back, teacher!" All of us straightened. One boy made a sound, and was quickly hushed by another. Miss Pointy raised an eyebrow and scratched it.

"How is it I'm supposed to watch my back? I haven't any eyes in my back." She seemed genuinely perplexed by the request. She even glanced over her shoulder, to see how it felt. "No, I'd never be able to watch my back and teach at the same time. Never." She shook her head sadly, and sighed. "Oh, well. Can't be helped. Note to self." She wrote on a pad on her desk. "Assign. Back. Watching. Monitor. Darrell? Darrell Sikes, isn't it? Would you mind watching my back for me, since you were initially kind enough to show concern in that regard? It would be the first assigned job of the school year."

He was confused. We were all confused. But we were smiling. Darrell was not.

"YES make life easy on yourself," Miss Pointy said. "Don't mess with your teacher. Speaking of making life easy and of messes, I need your help to lighten the daily load. First, may I have a volunteer to stay and help me after school, clean up the erasers and such? Someone from the neighborhood, no one who needs to catch the school bus, sorry. This is a permanent job. I'll call and get permission from your parents. Your name?"

"Rachel."

There went my walk home. Oh, well. I thought of raising my hand as she named other classroom jobs, ones that would rotate so we all would get a turn: messenger, homework returner, current-events reporter, on and on. Maybe she could use more help after school, maybe I could ask her and she would say yes and I could clean erasers with Rachel. But I hadn't raised my hand in *years*. I wasn't sure my hand still knew how to raise. I lifted my wrist limply. It wasn't going to happen.

"You'll be leaving before lunch today. Just enough time to pass out textbooks." Miss Pointy let out a little private laugh. "Any of you ever read a textbook under the blankets, with a flashlight?"

We looked at each other, then shook our heads.

"Anyone ever recommend a textbook to a friend? Did you ever say, 'This is so great! You've got to read this!'?"

No.

"Anyone cry at the end of a textbook?"

We laughed. No.

"Huh," said Miss Pointy. "Well, they make lovely paperweights anyway, don't you think? I'll find something else for us to read for the most part. Now, while I'm passing these out, as I'm mandated—"

"What's 'mandated'?"

"Bossed. You work in your new journals. Some days you will write about your life—"

"Bo-ring," someone called out.

Miss Pointy stopped cold. "Who said that?" Nobody answered. "Boring is a swear word in this class. I don't want to hear boring. Ever." She picked up a textbook, a heavy one, and slammed it on her desk. We all jumped. "If that word comes out of your mouth you will be sent down to the nurse. She'll give you a shot on your south side to cure your boringitis and send you home. You just test me once and see if I'm kidding. Understand? Anyone here not understand?" Her voice was low. She really looked angry. She was crazy. She walked a full circle around her desk and took a deep breath. "As I was *saying*, you will write about your life. If your life happens to be b-o-r-i-n-g," she spelled, "then you had better learn to make life a little more interesting, because I don't read anything b-o-r-i-n-g."

"Why not?" Raphael ventured.

"Because. It's . . . it's . . . b-o-r-i-n-g." The mood seemed to lift as suddenly as it had come. "Now. I've told you all about myself, haven't I? How my first husband was a pirate, and I'm using this job to supplement my night job selling encyclopedias, yadda-yadda-yadda? Now, I need you to tell me everything I need to know about *you*."

Everyone stared at her.

"Make hay while the sun shines! Today! *Go!*"

We all started writing, or asked to borrow something to write with. Miss Pointy rolled her eyes, passed out a School Supply List and a *Lista de Utencilios Escolares*. Soon everyone was either writing or chewing on their pens and looking like they were trying to see their eyebrows. Everyone except me. I stared at everyone in turn, imagining what they would write.

Rachel:

I really don't see why I should sit in the back row plus something you should know is I need new glasses only my mother has not taken me yet so I don't see why I must sit in the back row where I can hardly see so please teacher please please change my seat. Love your loving helper Rachel.

Or Darrell:

Somethin you shid no about me is I ant gon wach your back you wach your own back teecher p.s. you are stopid and ugly. and BORING BORING BORING BORING BORING BORING BORING

And then everyone else:

I like recess.

My big sister is going to have a baby in three months.

I want a Game Cube for my birthday.

I WANT A PET BUT IN MY BUILDING IT'S NO DOGS ALLOWED, NOT EVEN CATS.

Taco day is best in the lunchroom, but they don't give enough cheese.

I spend summers with my grandma in Alabama.

I like boys even though they can be sooo immature.

I have to go to the bathroom a lot, please don't yell at me.

soree techer, no speck inglish.

Then, I tried to think of what I wanted to say. I thought of saying how I was held back, but then I realized this wasn't something I wanted to say. I wanted to say I was sorry I made my mother feel so disappointed, but then I realized that was something I should say to my mother, not my teacher . . . and this, too, wasn't something I wanted to say. I wanted to tell Miss Pointy I am good at looking at things and smelling things and seeing things and touching things and hearing things and thinking things and remembering things, but so what? These aren't things that are important to know at school, are they? They don't fill in any blank, do they? So all these things I know are a secret, I keep them inside myself, in a box made of myself. Only I seem to have lost the key and now I don't know how to take it all out when I need it.

I wanted to tell the teacher that the world looks different from the second row, that I liked the flowers and the red lamp, and that I wished she knew I wanted to be a helper even though I didn't raise my hand. I wished she were a goldfish bowl turned upside down and could see me reflected in her, the way I want to be seen, without my having to tell her. I want to be seen in a way that takes her by surprise, upside down and backward from what's before her eyes.

The bell rang. A blank page stared up at me.

"Pass up your journals," she instructed. Kids started twisting around in their seats, collecting books from behind them. I felt panicked. I picked up my pen. I wrote:

I am a writer

And then my journal was one in a pile, being pushed forward. I could not tell which one was mine. I grew red and hot and foolish-feeling at the thought of Miss Pointy looking at those words. What was I thinking?

After all, in the end, she was going to be a teacher about it.

I am a writer

I believe you.

6

The Lion's Lesson

$\mathcal{M}$iss Pointy is . . . pointy. Her nose is pointy. Her ears are pointy. Her shoes are pointy. And boy, are her fingers ever pointy. Sometimes even her voice is pointy. Especially when she says *you*. The *you* she's usually talking to is Darrell Sikes. Darrell Sikes always has fire in his eyes. Anything Miss Pointy tells him, he looks at her like she just told him she ran over his dog. He makes these grunting sounds and talks under his breath, until Miss Pointy can't ignore it anymore. She takes him out in the hall, she thinks we can't hear, but we're real quiet then, so we can. She says things like, "I can't make you do anything, it's your choice, please help me," when she's not too frustrated, but when she's mad, she says things like,

"Keep talking to yourself all day in that crazy way, you're going to end up a crazy man sitting at the back of the public bus with dead pigeons in a Hefty bag! How's that sound?" I hear Darrell saying nothing, and I feel mixed up. I know that angry feeling of grown-ups trying to push their way into the room of your mind, and I know that feeling of trying to hold the door shut against them with quiet and looking down. But I knew why I was angry, at my teachers, at my counselor. I don't know why Darrell is angry. At everybody.

Miss Pointy tries to get us to leave our problems at home. She stands at the doorway every morning, smiling like she's auditioning to be a movie star, but she blocks the door and nobody gets in until they use the trouble basket. We pretend to put our troubles into the big green basket she holds out before we enter. Our troubles are invisible to the eye, but they are heavy. She practically breaks her back, holding all those troubles for us, but she says we can't carry them into the classroom ourselves or we won't be able to work. She offers the troubles back to us at the end of the day, since they don't belong to her. Nobody's ever taken them back. Still, they seem to follow us and find us at home, like black cats.

In class, Miss Pointy ignores Darrell's Special Needs. She calls on him the same as everyone else. She waits a long time for him to answer. Then we all have to wait.

"Darrell? I'm waiting on you." Silence. "'I don't know' is an acceptable answer."

"How 'bout 'I don't care'?" he sneered. As a class, we made a low moan.

"Less acceptable," said Miss Pointy, and continued to wait. And wait. Finally, she moved on.

"Stupid Miss Potty," Darrell grumbled.

"Yes, Darrell? You have something to say, now that your turn is over?" Miss Pointy grumbled back.

"You called me a *barrel*!" yelled Darrell. Some boys snorted through their noses, because Darrell *is* kind of round and solid, barrel-shaped. He crossed his arms and pouted.

"I certainly didn't call you a barrel, Darrell. Why would I call you a barrel?" She sighed. "Please stop talking crazy talk."

"You always calling me crazy!" he roared.

"You're always acting crazy!" she roared back.

Then Darrell got up, kicked Miss Pointy's desk, and sat back down, his chest heaving. I would have been afraid. Miss Pointy looked unhappy, but not afraid. She got up and stood next to Darrell's desk.

"Excuse me," she said. She kicked his desk firmly with her toe. He jumped. "Huh. Did kicking a desk work for you? It's not working for me."

"You're not kicking it hard enough," said Darrell sweetly.

"Mmmm," she nodded. "I see. Would you mind getting up again?" Darrell stood. She shooed him a few paces away, and then she picked up the hem of her long ballroom skirt just slightly before punting the desk so mightily that it tipped over with a terrific crash and slid about three feet.

We stared.

"Ouch," said Miss Pointy.

She took her foot out of her high-heeled shoe and rubbed her toe. Then she hobbled back to her own desk. "It still doesn't work for me. Well, thanks anyway, Darrell. Or Barrel. Or Feral. Or whatever it is you want people to call you. Now let's get back to work."

Darrell-Barrel was too pigheaded to go and get his desk so he had to do his work on his lap. When we came back from lunch, the desk was set right again.

The point of this story is, don't try to out-crazy a crazy.

You see, even Miss Pointy's stories have points. She likes to tell stories about foxes and crows a lot. Crows putting pebbles in jugs and making the cool water rise. Foxes snapping sharp jaws at grapes just out of reach, walking away, not caring. Dogs losing bones to reflections in the stream. Ants working, grasshoppers playing. She told us a story about a fox and a stork. The fox invites the stork for dinner, but serves food in a flat saucer, so the stork can't eat. The stork invites the fox to dinner, and for revenge serves food in a narrow-necked jar, so the fox can't eat. "What's the lesson here?" she asked.

"Foxes and storks don't know how to eat dinner," said Leon.

"Fox should of just ate stork," Angelina observed.

"Maybe he was still full," suggested Michael.

"When people aren't nice, everyone ends up hungry and suffering," Ernie said.

"Hmmm, that's a good one." Miss Pointy rubbed her chin.

"No, it ain't!" argued Leon. "There's no people, just foxes and storks."

"When you go to someone else's house, sometimes they don't serve what you like," offered Mariah.

"Yeah! I slept over at Veronica's, and her momma served government cheese!" said Sakiah. Veronica turned around and sent Sakiah a stabbing look. "Well, she did!"

"Girl, your mouth is as big as a saucer!" Raphael laughed. "Come on, Miss Pointy. Tell us what's the lesson."

"Tit for tat," said Miss Pointy. This sent Raphael and some of the boys into such uncontrollable giggles, she sent them out of the room, one at a time, to the water fountain.

"That story nasty, Miss Pointy," said Dominique upon his return.

"I didn't make up these stories, you know. Aesop did."

"Why he always writing about animals?" demanded Kiarre. "Didn't he know no people?"

"He *was* writing about people. He gave the animals the qualities he saw in people: bitterness, perseverance, foolishness, trickery, pride. But Aesop had certain qualities, too, that made it so he had to tell stories for survival. He was a slave to King Xanthus, in ancient Greece. He was *mute*, he couldn't talk. He was ugly. They say he had a humped back, bowed legs, a potbelly, and he was short as a dwarf."

"Dang! That *is* ugly!" Tanaeja agreed.

"The Greek gods looked upon him and didn't just see what was on the outside. They saw he was decent on the inside. So they gave him the gifts of speech and storytelling. Do you think those were good gifts?"

"I'd rather be handsome," Larry admitted.

"Would you have known Aesop was ugly if I hadn't told you?"

No, we shook our heads. "He writes handsome stories," said Rashonda.

"I think so, too. He used his stories to advise the king. Sometimes he disagreed with the king's way of thinking, but he couldn't say so outright, or guess what?"

"They'd kill him!" We cheered.

"Off with his head!" Sakiah shouted.

"You gotta watch The Man," warned Dominique.

Miss Pointy did not argue. "Instead of disagreeing with the king, he used his stories to offer the bit of common sense the king might have been missing. Maybe he used animals so the story wouldn't seem too personal."

"He tricked him!" Ernie said.

"*Persuaded.*" Miss Pointy winked.

Then she told us a fable she said was one of her favorites, about a lion trapped in a net, who is chewed out to freedom by a little mouse. She asked what the story showed.

"Be careful of traps, whether you're a mouse or a lion," said Ernie.

"That's a good piece of advice for a king," said Miss Pointy, nodding.

"Or if you're a mouse or a lion," added Ernie emphatically.

"You gotta watch The Man," suggested Dominique.

"Perhaps," Miss Pointy said, "but please try to think of a new lesson, Dominique. That was not the moral of all of Aesop's fables."

Dominique slumped down in his seat, blushing. "I'm just *saying*," he muttered. "Ya'll better *watch* him."

"That's your daddy's moral, not Aesop's," laughed Tanaeja.

"You be quiet about my daddy!" Dominique said.

"Now, now, stay on business. What's the lesson of the story?"

"Pay back favors," said Ameer.

"Good," said Miss Pointy, smiling. "Anyone else?"

"It doesn't matter if someone is different, they can be your friend and help you when you need it most," said Paris. She was smart. Miss Pointy took out her Happy Box, a little box full of stickers she takes out sometimes if you impress her. We moaned, jealous.

"Paris is right. No one is so weak that on occasion he can't be a help to you. That's what Aesop meant, so that Xanthus shouldn't overlook the smaller countries in efforts to make alliances," explained Miss Pointy.

"What's 'alliances'?"

"Friendships. If there's a *conflict*, a war, you need all the friends you can get."

"If you're in a war, we'll be your allies," Ernie spoke for all of us. Almost all of us. Darrell had been quiet, burning his look into Miss Pointy's forehead all along, silently crushing his teeth against each other inside his mouth. I could see his jaw moving.

"I'll be counting on it," said Miss Pointy. "Let's write in our journals now."

I imagined what Darrell would write. Later I

was able to see, because it was my turn to check in homework on the chart. I stayed after with Rachel and peeked when Miss Pointy took the rest of the class out.

"I don't think you should look in people's journals," said Rachel.

"Just one person's, I promise," I said.

"Whose?""

"Darrell's."

She laughed. "You're crazy. He probably can't even write."

"Come on. Want to see?"

She leaned over, but then pulled back. "No," she said. "Curiosity killed the cat."

What a way to die, I thought. "Did Aesop say that?"

"No, your momma did. Get in trouble by your-self, cuz. I'd like to get out of the fifth grade." She went back to cleaning the board in wide, wet lines with a sponge. I read.

She a bich a big one why she go sayin
that I ant never sed nothin to her ima
tell my moma then will see

Well, I wasn't too far off.

"What'd it say?" she asked.

I thought curiosity killed the cat? "You were right," I said. "It's nothing."

7

George Gets Busted

After lunch we push the desks to the sides of the room and gather in the middle. Then, there in the soft rosy glow of her lamp, Miss Pointy shares stories with us. Miss Pointy says some stories are for reading and some stories are for telling. She told us the story about George Washington. He cut down a cherry tree, and then his momma came and said, "Boy, did *you* do this?" And he said, "Yeah," which I thought was stupid, and so did everybody else.

"Was he holding the ax when his momma come?" Raphael asked.

"I don't know. Probably."

"Busted!"

"Dang! He should of put the ax down and said he didn't know nothing about it."

"She would have known he was lying," said Miss Pointy. "She was his mother."

"Yeah, but she couldn't *prove* it."

"She didn't have to prove it. She was his *mother*," she repeated. "Do you have to prove everything to your mother, or does she just know?" Miss Pointy was looking so exactly the other way of Darrell that I knew she was thinking about him. "George Washington went on to become the first president of the United States."

The class was silent.

"So?" came a voice.

"Excuse me?"

"I mean, so what?" shrugged Raphael. "I don't get it. He chopped down a tree, he was busted, and then he became president. I repeat," he said, smiling, "*so?*"

"For one thing, he wasn't *busted*," Miss Pointy explained. "He had the chance to tell the truth, and he did. People tell that story because it showed he was an honest man, and that's what the American people wanted: an honest man. I tell this story to you because I think that same quality of honesty will get you far in life. Honesty isn't even really the right word, I think it's more like *accountability.*" She got up and wrote the word on the blackboard. We couldn't see it in the dim light, but we could hear the tapping of the chalk. "Accountability means, if you've got the guts to do something, at least have the guts to say you've done it."

"How come we don't have presidents like that no more?" asked Raphael.

"Maybe you'll have to bring it back in style," Miss Pointy said so matter-of-factly, we all turned to smile at Raphael at once, and then we laughed. It wasn't a making-fun-of laugh, it was a gentle, embarrassed laugh, like we all saw the secret part of him for a second, the part that showed him all grown up, not just a smart aleck, but a man with a job.

"I don't want to be president!" His face was turning red, like the idea was buzzing around his head like a fly and frustrating him. "Anyway, the story's not true."

"Maybe it's true, maybe it's not, it doesn't matter," said Miss Pointy.

"What do you mean, it doesn't matter?" Angelina forgot to raise her hand. "The whole story is about telling the truth. How can you say it doesn't matter whether the story is true or not?"

"True things don't always happen in the world, where you can see and touch them. True things also happen in the imagination." I stared at her as she said this amazing thing so easily, as though she were telling us the time. "If it happened that somebody was living a life that made him wish for an honest man, so he made up that story, then there's something true about that story, even if the events didn't really happen. Do you see?"

I wanted to see, because I wanted to be like Miss Pointy, a woman who loved stories even better than TV. So I thought about this. I watched as some of my classmates pretended to think about this, but really were watching other people think about this.

"So, if it's not a true story about a man being accountable, it's a true story about somebody *wishing* a man was accountable?" I said as I raised my hand. I had to speak slowly. My mind felt like it was trying to carry a shallow pie pan full of water, and if I wasn't careful, it would splash and spill. The class looked at me like they looked at Raphael, but they didn't laugh. What were they seeing in me?

Miss Pointy was looking at me, too, tenderly, like a mother who doesn't need her child to prove anything, but is just glad to know what that child is made of.

"We can turn on the lights now," is all she said. "Time to write in our journals."

True things don't always happen in
the world, where you can see and touch
them
    True things also happen in the
imagination
    I raised my hand today in both places

I didn't get a chance to write more than that because the door opened and there was Darrell's momma. "I've got words for you." She pointed a crooked finger at Miss Pointy and stepped forward.

Miss Pointy asked, "Did you stop in the office for a pass?"

Darrell's momma said, "I'm not going to stop at any office, I'm going to speak to you right *now.*"

"Surely you can see, I'm in the middle of teaching a roomful of children," she said, real calm. I wrote the word *surely* lightly on the cover of my folder, in pencil, to surely use sometime.

Darrell's momma eyed Miss Pointy up and down, wrinkling up her nose at her fluffy dress. "I don't care what you in the middle of," Darrell's momma said. "You called my son a jackass in front of the whole class."

We didn't dare to breathe.

"I don't know where you got that idea." Miss Pointy looked at Luz and her eyes pointed silently to the wall. Luz got up and pressed the button twice, to signal the office for an emergency. Luz can be such a goody-two-shoes. But this time I was glad.

"You calling my son a liar?"

"Class?" Miss Pointy looked at us as if she had just asked us a review question.

"She never called him a jackass, and I have perfect attendance, so I know." Sakiah's squeaky voice came from the back. "He's the one always calling out her name and not doing his work, just messing around."

Dominique stood up. He is bigger than Darrell, so he's not scared of him. "He called her Miss Potty, but that ain't her name. It's Miss PWAH-TEE-YAY, it rhymes with a French word that means 'gotcha.'"

"Actually, 'you got me,'" Miss Pointy corrected him. "Thank you, Dominique."

Darrell's momma looked around at us slowly, but none of us said anything more. Then Darrell's momma marched right over to Darrell's desk, which was only about four steps away, because Miss Pointy keeps him in the front row. Darrell's momma took the journal off of Darrell's desk and whacked him over his skull, yelling, "Maybe you *are* a jackass!"

Miss Pointy stepped up and snatched the journal out of Darrell's momma's hand quick as a ninja and whacked her once on the hands, real sharp.

Darrell's momma's mouth made a shape like she was trying to inhale a hard-boiled egg.

"We don't swear in my classroom. Hardly ever. And we don't hit. Much." Just then, the door opened, and there was the vice-principal.

"Is there a problem, ladies?"

"Children. Excuse us for a moment. Please, continue to write in your journals. Maybe write the moral of the story," Miss Pointy said hurriedly, as they stepped out into the hall.

The door closed. We were too scared to speak. Most of us.

"The moral is, mind your cherry tree, George Washington," Dominique growled at Darrell. "I'll kick your behind till you look like Aesop, lying and bringing your crazy momma in here like that."

"Dominique, be quiet," hissed Tanaeja. "Ain't nobody in here be talking 'bout nobody's momma."

"Anyway, that isn't the moral of the story," said Kiarre calmly, bigger than all of us and afraid of nothing. "The moral is just what Miss Pointy said. 'Stop in the office for a pass.'"

This satisfied us, and we didn't speak any more. Darrell didn't look up. He was writing in his journal, like Miss Pointy asked. I started thinking about him. How does it feel to have a momma who doesn't know anything about you? A momma who needs you to prove whether or not you're a liar, who doesn't just know?

One thing for sure, Darrell Sikes makes school more interesting.

I know it's nosy, but I couldn't wait until I had another chance to see his journal. I hoped it had a *sorry* in it.

She a bich why she hit me in front of the hole class I dint do NOTHIN and futhumore why dint miss POTTY POTTY POTTY say nothin bout callin me baril, she so foney. P.S. Domaneek better whach his tale Im gon whip him bad.

As I mentioned to your mother, we do not swear in class. You will write "bitch" ten times so you learn to spell

it correctly and then I will never see
it or hear it from you again. School
language, please.

Miss Potty
(only you may call me that, then
we'll call it even)

speekin of LANGWAGE Miss oo-la-
la why don't you speek eenglish, this is
the younited states of america not planit
of the apes. You talk fancy but I no a
secrit, you ant all that MISS POTTY

Darrell, see me during recess this
week, I'm going to teach you the
brand of English I speak. I'm invit-
ing Dominique, so you won't be lonely. You don't have to thank me.

Miss Oo-la-la
(beats Miss Potty any day)

8

The Way Things Are Built

Miss Pointy loves to show us slides of the way things are built. She says it's *architecture*. The way Miss Pointy talks about architecture, it's as if it is a person, something built from the inside out. She gave us drinking straws to try to construct what we think the skeletons of skyscrapers look like. "Beams are the bones that hold the body," she said. While we worked, she showed us black-and-white photographs of men balancing on these beams, eating lunch, talking, at home in the sky. The sky is definitely Somewhere Else. Looking at these men, I thought about Heaven. I wondered if my father was working construction.

This arch in Paris, France. That dome in Florence, Italy. This wall, that pillar, this doorway, that window. Miss Pointy pointed out details in stone that looked like piped whipped cream. She showed us palaces, cliff dwellings, tipis, shanties, barns. Fountains, filigrees, spires, gargoyles watching from on high, stairs, pillars, bridges. I love these words, I couldn't write them down fast enough, magic words that bring your mind to Somewhere Else. But they aren't all somewhere else. Some of them are right here in Chicago. She showed us pictures of our own city. The Bahá'í Temple, Wrigley Field, the Water Tower, the Tribune building. She showed us the beautiful stones in the Graceland cemetery. She showed us the pink Edgewater Beach apartments off of Lake Shore Drive near Bryn Mawr, from the days when Uptown had movie studios and fine hotels. She showed us the skyline of Navy Pier, the long jetty with its elegant Ferris wheel slowly turning amid the seagulls. She said she would take us to see Buckingham Fountain at night when the weather gets warm, she said she'd treat us all to *churros* and we could watch the colors change in the water. She said we would all go to the bathroom at the Palmer House Hotel.

She said she would take us to the top of the Sears Tower someday. We were afraid, but we didn't mention it exactly.

"Grandma says skyscrapers is a sin, it's bad for man to try to reach God," Angelina said.

"I think it's a sin not to try," said Miss Pointy. "If we are all God's children, as your grandmother would probably say, then isn't it natural for a child to reach up to a parent?"

I knew the answer. But then I had another question: isn't it just as natural for a parent to reach for his child? When I thought of my father's architecture, I hung my head and closed my eyes. In my imagination I heard the roar of heavy machinery approaching, I felt the walls of myself shimmy and crack. Even though I told myself it was in my head, I had to hold on to my desk for a minute, a hand tight on each side, thinking the words I didn't write.

Dear Daddy, My heart is a shanty. So why did you send a wrecking ball? Why didn't you build me a house instead, or a skyscraper a million stories high?

The only stories I can build are on paper, but I thought of that hungry file cabinet in the counselor's office and I didn't dare write anything here at school. In my mind's eye, I wrote the letter to my father. In my mind's eye, I crumpled that letter into a ball.

Then the sound I imagined rolls away. I blinked, and I was surprised to see walls still standing all around me. Everyone but me was building skyscrapers.

"Finish your structures for homework," said Miss Pointy.

Everyone finishes their homework for Miss Pointy, because Miss Pointy gives beautiful glittery stickers for prizes. Luz gets a lot of stickers from Miss Pointy. I am not the sticker police, I just know this because I sit right behind her to the left. I couldn't help but notice how after a short time had passed, her collection had spread all over the front of her journal like measles. Then it was so full, she had to start putting them on the inside cover.

"Doesn't that make your journal kind of heavy?" I asked.

"Eees okay." Luz smiled at me. "I don mind."

Whenever a paper is passed back, I see Luz bounce just a little bit on her bottom, she's so excited. Then she takes her fingernail and goes pick-pick-pick at the corner of the sticker until it comes off of her paper, and she re-sticks it on her journal cover. Luz isn't all that smart, but she gets them anyway, because Miss Pointy says trying your best is a success in itself.

What does that make me? I don't have a single sticker.

Once Miss Pointy saw that Luz's cover was filled and she said, "When I was a little girl, I collected stickers, too," and they smiled at each other. I guess I wasn't the only one who overheard this gross conversation, because then all the girls and some of the boys started peeling stickers off their papers and sticking them on their journals. But I'll bet two bags of chips Miss Pointy brought her old collection from home and secretly gave it to Luz, because Luz suddenly turned up with glossy photo-album pages of stars and hearts and unicorns and what-all. I also think Miss Pointy secretly gave Ernie a book of Aesop's Fables, too. For keeps! I complained to Rachel about this.

"I don't want a book of Aesop's Fables." She shrugged.

"Even if she offered it to you?"

"She didn't offer it to me. She offered it to Ernie. I guess she must have been tired of him asking for the same old stories over and over." I must have been looking grumpy, because Rachel added, "I think it was nice of her. Don't be jealous."

"Jealous!" There was no use talking to Rachel. I suppose she also thought it was nice that Miss Pointy gave Boris the same book, even though he doesn't speak a word of English, not one word! Ernie can go over to Boris's desk and look at the book with him whenever he wants, he doesn't even have to ask, he just goes, and there they are, Miss Pointy doesn't even look up.

This class has class pets.

I wanted to write, *Why does some girl who just learned to speak English two years ago get twenty million stickers, while I get zero?* But then I remembered what Miss Pointy's answer would be. She even wrote it in my journal, in red ink, after I hadn't done a journal entry in four days straight.

A writer writes.

Why can't she be normal and say "Do your work" like any other teacher? Why can't she take me out in the hall like I was Darrell Sikes and tell me that I'm capable of so much more, talk about disappointment and calling my mother and grades? But no, she's trickier than that. A *writer writes*, she says. Like she's saying, *Are you writing, or are you nobody?* That's the way it feels.

Maybe she doesn't mean it like that, maybe she's just giving matter-of-fact writing advice, like she always does in my journal. I understand some of it, like

> *If you hear a good word that belongs to someone else, write it down somewhere so it belongs to you, too.*

I already do that. What's she telling me that for?

> *Don't ever end a story, "And then I woke up. It was just a dream!" That's a very cheap trick.*

> *Don't kill your characters. The worst ones should go on and on and on, just like in real life.*

Some of her comments I don't understand very well.

Kid vs. nature, kid vs. kid, kid vs. himself. Pick a fight.

Words that don't mean much: nice, pretty, ugly, bad, good.

Know how to tell who's the main character? It's not always the one you like the best. It's the one who changes.

During journal time, I stare at her words, moving each piece of advice in my mind like a hand explores a stone in a collection of stones. But the same one stands out every time: "A writer writes." This is not a stone, this is a rock, and I don't want it. I just want a sticker, and I know she'd give me a thousand stickers if I would only do my work. But I'm no begging dog. I can buy me all the stickers I want at the store.

I taste the flavor of sour grapes, like the fox on the cover of Ernie's book of fables. I swallow it down.

Usually Miss Pointy hands back the journals, but one bad day she was busy fixing some equipment in the back of the room, so she let Leon pass the journals back. He wasn't paying attention and gave them to all the wrong people. A star-covered journal appeared on my desk. I quickly slid it under my desk and into my lap, and stared at the collection of bears and clowns and unicorns and brightly colored words:

GOOD JOB!

YOU CAN DO IT!

FAR OUT!

I'M IMPRESSED!

In the left corner was a star with a rainbow streaming behind it. All that glitters is not gold, says Aesop, but if it was gold glitter, that was good enough for me. I felt my finger tweaking at one of the star's points, only it wasn't my finger, it was a robot's finger, programmed to do some other, bad girl's bidding. I felt the useless resistance of the sticker, trying to stay on poor Luz's notebook. The star curled away.

Luz raised her hand, waved it, panicked. "Mees Pointee! Thees ees not my journal!"

"This isn't mine, either," said Ernie.

"Well, don't open them! They're private!" Everyone opened them. "Darrell! Sakiah! Hey! Close those books!" Miss Pointy directed, turning away from the VCR to confiscate the journals. "I'll pass them back myself. Heavens, Leon, can't I count on you?" I felt Luz's notebook being lifted from my grasp. I hadn't had a chance to put the star back. I meant to. I was just seeing how sticky it was. My journal was handed back to me. I stuck the star on the inside cover. I glanced over at Luz. She was looking at the cover of her journal, then she began to crane her neck. Would she raise her hand? No, she just leaned back hard in her chair, and slowly ran her fingers across the stickers she had left. Plenty of stickers, in my opinion. She didn't write anything, she just made fists and rested her cheeks on them. She frowned.

"Wanna see what I wrote in my journal?" Paris offered, tapping my shoulder from behind across the aisle. I was surprised.

"Sure," I said.

I read:

Miss Pointy, Please DO read.
IMPORTANT!!!
Luz's collection isn't the only
sticky thing in this room. Someone
has STICKY FINGERS. Just thought you
should know.

Mom says, in the city, there's a million windows. Someone's always watching you, seeing what you are doing, what's happening to you. It always made me feel safe, like wherever I was, I had guardian angels. I realized, suddenly, that maybe other people have guardian angels, too. I handed the journal back to Paris, careful to keep my mouth a straight, closed line. Then I couldn't help it. I turned back to Paris and opened my mouth.

"What do you want?" I hissed.

"Not a thing." She smiled innocently. Paris plays with Luz on the playground every day. Luz's best friend, kitty-corner behind me! How could I have been so careless!

"I was going to give it back," I turned around again.

"So give it," Paris folded her hands.

"Stop acting so grown-up," I growled.

"Sahara? Is there a problem?" Miss Pointy asked from the back of the room. "Please stop turning around and get to work. You, too, Paris."

Paris's smile makes me think I am going to go crazy.

We were supposed to write about architecture where we live. I stared at my blank page. Finally I wrote,

Do teachers have secrets?

That's all I wrote. Certainly not enough to earn a sticker. Suddenly, I realized I couldn't hand this journal back up to Miss Pointy, not with the star on the inside cover. So I peeled it off. It ripped a little, and curled into a coil. What should I do with it? I wondered. I didn't know, so I dropped it on the floor. From the corner of my eye, I saw Paris dip down to get it. Time went slowly.

Finally, Miss Pointy started collecting the

journals. Paris half-stood, reaching over my desk. "Here, Luz!" she called.

Luz took it, but she did not look happy. "Eees dirty. There's dirt all over eet," she remarked. "Why you take eet, Paris?"

Paris looked shocked. "Me!"

"I thought we were friends," she said to Paris.

"I didn't take it," said Paris.

"Then who deed?" Luz raised her hand. Paris seemed frozen, searching for her breath. Finally, she glared at me, set back down and crossed her arms.

"Yes, Luz?" Miss Pointy turned. I braced myself.

"I need some escotch tape," said Luz. "One of my esteekers ees loose."

Miss Pointy frowned, and got some clear Con-Tact paper. She showed Luz how to cover her whole book with the film. "Now, none of them will come off," she explained. Luz looked up gratefully. "I'm sorry I didn't think of it sooner."

Me, too, I thought.

At recess, Paris marched up to me.

"You gonna take care of your business or not?"

I couldn't even look at Paris in the eye.

"Cordelia told me you were bad, but I didn't believe her. I told her I like to make up my own mind. I thought we could be friends. Thanks, Sahara." She clucked her tongue, disgusted. I saw her feet turn and walk away.

I watched Paris and Luz make careful circles as they played, not crossing each other's paths. I leaned against the chain-link fence with Rachel, who said nothing, as usual. I had a conversation with myself, instead. More of a lecture. About how I read all those books, wishing life could be like what I read, wishing there would be such things as heroes and adventures. But a hero is the one who does what's hard, like Paris, taking the blame and losing a friend. Or Luz, saying words in another language, a language her own mother doesn't speak. Could I do what she does, take a risk with every word? The answer made my cheeks feel hot.

I looked at Kiarre, overgrown and pushy, trying so hard to be the policewoman instead of the criminal. Raphael, with his big mouth, wanting to laugh even if it's at himself. I thought about Ernie, hiding from the gangs in the library after school, and being called a chicken. Sakiah, telling on everyone and talking too much, tagging along like everybody's little sister. Even Darrell, beaten in front of the whole class, held back, mean and slow but present, every day; is school still better than home? He was a hero, too. *They told me you were bad, Darrell, but I didn't believe them. I like to make up my own mind. I thought we could be friends....*

I looked at my classmates, sprawled across the playground, their noise swirling all around me. I *like my class*, I thought, surprised. Aside from Cordelia, the rest of them were decent, not one of them had yet mentioned how I was held back, not one of them called me stupid or slow. They could have, couldn't they? What do they see, us girls against the chain-link fence? Is Rachel a shy girl, or a snob? Am I a mysterious girl, a secret-keeper, or just a thief, a girl who steals other people's rewards, telling herself she could earn them herself if she really wanted? If she really wanted! I turned away, my back to everyone, and closed my eyes tight.

Rachel noticed. "Are you okay?" I shook my head violently. I thought of saying, *Let's play with everyone else. Let's not stand here, by ourselves.* But I couldn't, not today. I knew I was standing where I belonged.

Before we entered the classroom, I whispered to Miss Pointy, "I need the trouble basket." She motioned to me with her finger, and pulled it out from under her desk. She held it low, by her knees, so it was private. I pretended to put my troubles in it. I put and I put and I put, while she watched silently, holding the handle with both hands. Then I looked at her and nodded that I was through.

I went back to my seat. My stomach had started to hurt. I put my head down and hid in the dark of my own arms. Miss Pointy didn't call on me for the rest of the day.

9

Miss Pointy Gets Me Where I Live

Rachel's brother, Freddie, was to blame for our stomach flu. Rachel and I were taking turns holding him, cuddling him, kissing him. He's so chubby, like a baby doll, we couldn't resist. Until he started throwing up. Then we handed him back to my aunt. Two days later, Rachel and I were throwing up, too.

We were lying with our feet sticking in each other's faces on the sofa in my living room. Rachel's momma couldn't take off any more work, so my mom took a sick day to take care of us. The hours passed slowly. The drone of cartoons had become wearisome, and the flickering of the screen began to nauseate us. Freddie drooled in his playpen, not knowing or caring what he had done to us with his evil, germy cuteness.

We tried entertaining ourselves by drawing pictures of each other. I stared at Rachel. Her hair looked like the Bride of Frankenstein. Her eyes had half-moons of green underneath, and the corners of her mouth had little fans of spittle. I didn't mention this. I imagined I looked the same. We showed each other our unimpressive work.

"Now what do you want to do?" I asked her.

"I don't know." Rachel shrugged.

We lay there, weak and staring at each other, thinking the word that Miss Pointy had trained us not to dare to say aloud. B-o-r-i-n-g.

"Let's eat toast," I suggested. We ate our toast, crust first, then middle.

"Ooogh," said Rachel.

"Mom!" I called.

Mom came running in. She put her arms around Rachel, and walked her to the bathroom. Strange, painful, wet cries drifted down the hallway. Pungent smells, and then the sound of teeth being brushed, the toilet being flushed, Lysol being sprayed. Rachel was walked back after a time, looking like Kiarre had given her the once-over.

"Oooogh," said Rachel.

"Now what do you want to do?" I asked.

"Sahara! Leave her be," Mom said, pulling over a pail within puke-shot. "Do you need one of these, too?"

"No, I don't think so," I said. "I feel okay. Except when I look at *her*."

Rachel smiled from the other end of the sofa, her eyes closed. Then she frowned, and leaned over the pail. She made some noises, but nothing came out.

"Don't excite her. Read a book. Read to her. Do something quietly."

"Her toes are about two million degrees," I complained. "I think I'm getting blisters where her toes are touching my leg."

My mother felt Rachel's head. "Oh, honey," she said, and got some Tylenol. Rachel swallowed the pills, and took noisy, experimental sips from a glass of water. Mom and I watched with interest. Nothing came up. "Try to sleep, boo-boo." Then she turned to me. "You let her sleep," she warned.

After Mom left the room, Rachel lay there

with a cool rag on her forehead, moaning exotically. "Let's pretend you're sick," I suggested.

"I am sick," she reminded me.

"No, really sick. We're sisters, lost in the desert."

"Nnnngghhh. Too hot."

"All right, the tundra. I'm nursing you back to health on seal blubber and fish."

Rachel leaned over the pail.

"Sahara!" My mother's voice scolded from the kitchen.

I whispered. "It seems like you're close to the end, but don't go on that ice drift, Rachel-Quiet-River-Flowing. Your betrothed, Darrell-Whose-Mother-Pounds, will be heartbroken." Rachel eyed me from over the pail.

"Make it Dominique," she croaked, leaning back into the pillows.

I waited for her to ask me who I liked. The question never came.

"I am your older sister. I have to get married first," I explained. "Who will it be?"

Rachel snored delicately at the other end of the sofa. Freddie shifted in the playpen, sucking on the paw of his worn-out teddy bear. I sighed, and picked up *Julie of the Wolves*. Time moved more quickly with my book friends than my real friends, I noticed, a little sadly.

The doorbell rang. I heard my mother say, "Who is it?" into the intercom.

"Madame Poitier," said the voice. "Miss Pointy."

"Miss Pointy?" My mom couldn't hide her surprise. She buzzed her in. I buried myself under the blanket and closed my eyes. I couldn't stand to see Miss Pointy, not after stealing Luz's sticker, even if she didn't know it was me. And then getting sick! And missing school! It was too embarrassing, too weak. I flopped my arm over the side of the sofa.

"Sahara?" Mom came in. I tried to breathe evenly. Mom clucked her tongue, believing I was asleep. She went to the door.

"Ms. Jones?" I heard Miss Pointy's voice at the door. "Is Sahara here? I brought her homework."

"That was nice of you," said Mom. "Especially since she doesn't do it, does she?"

"Well, it's still hers, to do or not do."

"I guess so," said Mom. "She and Rachel are

sleeping. Won't you come in? Or are you on your way somewhere? Special?" I supposed Mom had just noticed her wardrobe. Miss Pointy must have been wearing one of her party dresses. Or maybe her sparkling tiara. Or her ankle-length leopard-skin coat? I opened one eye, but couldn't see anything.

"I just came from somewhere special," said Miss Pointy.

"I thought you were coming from school."

"I am."

"Oh," said Mom.

"I'm sorry to intrude. I just wanted to drop this off. I know you weren't expecting me. . . ."

"That's fine. I've been home with three sick kids all day, I'm so *bored*." I cringed at the B-word. "Come in for just a few minutes. I have marble cake," said Mom.

I wondered if Mom had her by the arm. The door closed, and I heard the footsteps into the kitchen, the next room over. I heard the kettle bang on the burner. I heard the women sitting together, Mom taking drags on her cigarette.

"Smoke?"

"No, thanks."

"Did you quit?"

"I never quit anything," Miss Pointy said. "I just finish."

"I wish I could finish smoking," said Mom.

"Finish what you start," said Miss Pointy. *Good grief,* I thought, *how do teachers ever have friends outside of school, if they always talk like teachers?* Mom just laughed.

"You're a real teacher, aren't you," she said. "Having any luck with Sahara this year?"

"What do you mean?"

"I mean, considering her history. You read her records, didn't you?"

"No," said Miss Pointy. "I hate reading records. I never do it, until the end of the year. Then it's fun. You can see if other people think you're right or wrong." Mom must have been giving her a strange look, because she kept explaining. "If a kid is wild, or slow, or can't read, it'll show in good time. I have eyes. I don't need those records."

"Seems the records would save time, though."

"Not if they're wrong."

The kettle sang. "So you haven't seen Sahara's file, huh," said Mom.

"Nope. I just see Sahara."

"Well. What do you see?" I knew Mom was holding her breath a little bit. So was I.

"She is going to be a writer," said Miss Pointy. I felt myself blow up suddenly, like a balloon that just had been attached to a helium tank.

"Is she?" Mom finally breathed. "What else?"

"Sorry," said Miss Pointy. "That's all I know about her right now. She doesn't show me a lot."

"Does she write for you?"

"No, not really," said Miss Pointy. "This is good tea."

"Then why do you say she's a writer?"

"I didn't say she was a writer. I said she's going to be a writer. A writer writes. When she starts writing, she'll be a writer," Miss Pointy explained.

"Oh." Mom sounded annoyed. "Well, maybe when she starts practicing rocket science, she'll be a rocket scientist."

"Maybe," agreed Miss Pointy in a muffled voice. It sounded like her mouth was full of cake.

"Except I don't think she's going to be a rocket scientist. I think she's going to be a writer."

"Well, what should I do with this great talent?"

"Read to her. Even though she's a big girl. Leave a lot of pens and paper around the house. Give her a lot of books to read to herself. Probably stuff you've been doing all along."

"You really haven't read the file, have you?" Mom marveled. I thought I heard a little relief in her voice. "You know, she's been held back."

"It'll be great material," said Miss Pointy, her mouth full again. "Great artists suffer. She keeps a journal at school, you know."

"She does?" said Mom. "Can I read it?"

"I lent her the money for the journal. She owes me two bucks," Miss Pointy said abruptly. "Can you advance her?"

"Now?"

"Now's good."

I wondered what Mom's face looked like, fetching the money from her purse.

"Can I read it?" Mom repeated.

"Sorry. Her debt's paid. It's her journal now. You've got to ask her," said Miss Pointy.

"I bought her a notebook too, you know," Mom told her, lowering her voice. "She keeps it in between her mattresses. I sneak to look at it. It's just blank pages and pages ripped out."

Mom!

"*Tsk, tsk.* Maybe she knows you're snooping. Don't be embarrassed. I like snooping, too," Miss Pointy confessed. *Me, too,* I thought. "But either way, she wouldn't rip out blank pages, would she? She's probably writing something on them."

"Like letters," said Mom. I felt a pang.

"Sure. Or stories," said Miss Pointy. "Could be anything, really."

"She does love stories. Reads all the time, here at home," Mom tattled. "She'd rather read than play outside. She'd rather read than go anywhere." *Well, that's not true. Why do you think I read? To go everywhere.* "She's got a great vocabulary, too. She could talk to the queen of England."

"You don't have to sell me, Ms. Jones," said Miss Pointy. "I believe you. That's great."

The women sipped their tea. "Are you going to fail her?" Mom asked finally.

"Oh, I've never failed a child," said Miss Pointy cheerfully. "She, on the other hand, might fail herself."

"Maybe I failed her," Mom said quietly. I bit my lip, hearing Mom's voice tremble. "She's a good girl, she's just a little freaked out. Sometimes she still comes in my room, in the middle of the night. Is that normal, at her age?"

Mom! Do you have to tell her everything?

"I guess, if she's freaked out," said Miss Pointy.

Mom didn't seem to be listening. "Stuck in the apartment all day, you know how it is in the city. Maybe I could have made a better home, worked things out with her father. . . ."

"Excuse me," Miss Pointy broke in. "May I be perfectly honest? You're a class act, Ms. Jones, and you have nothing to feel bad about. I'll put it in your permanent record, if you like. *Good mother. Serves tea and cake without prompting. Just a little freaked out. See Sahara Jones for further details.*"

My mom laughed, but it crackled, like it

might have been a choice between that and crying. "I see why the children like you," said Mom.

"Compliments make me break out in a rash," said Miss Pointy. "Please tell Sahara to get well soon. Rachel, too."

After Miss Pointy left, Mom came in and dropped the homework on the coffee table and went back into the kitchen. I could hear her singing along with the radio.

I tried to go to sleep for real, not because I felt tired, but because I felt sad. Failing other people, I could just say "Sorry," but it hadn't occurred to me that I was failing myself. I didn't want to fail myself. I wouldn't know how to apologize for it. I sat up. Hidden in the pile of homework was my journal. I decided to do the assignment Miss Pointy had given us the day I stole Luz's sticker.

Where I Live
    I live in the city. I wonder what it's like, to live in the suburbs or the country. I imagine if you live in a house, it's easier because you have a yard or a bike and when your mom

sends you on an errand, she doesn't stare out the window till you get back and you don't have to run. I wonder what it's like, not to hear sirens and yelling, not to hear your neighbors. When Mr. Martinez who lives below us comes home from the factory in the middle of the night, he gives himself a wel-come-home party by putting on his Cuban music so loud, his music is full of trumpets and drums and the word corazón, corazón all the time. His music shakes like a bad woman. His music is a bigger woman than his wife, who is small boned, who I imagine is frowning in her housedress because he's sitting on the sofa drinking with his favorite woman. I think this as I watch the crystals on the old light fixture quiver from the throb of his corazón. His coming home is really something.

It's something to me, too. It's someone coming home. I listen for my mother, in the other room. Is she sleeping? Or is she waiting, too? Sometimes I go to her room, but she usually sends me back. She says her bed's too small. She says, Put a pretty picture in your mind's eye, you'll fall asleep, you won't be scared. You don't need me.

So I go back and lie down and listen to Mrs. Rosen, in the apartment above us. Shuffle, shuffle, thump. Shuffle, shuffle, thump. The thump is her cane. I hear her move to the kitchen. The chair scrapes against the linoleum. What is she doing in the kitchen, in the middle of the night? She's nice, she smiles at me on the street, she gave me a butter-scotch candy out of her handbag with the little gold clasp. When she gave it to me, I looked at her hands, wrinkled with more lines than a road map, speckled with lakes of brown. What is it like to be old, I wonder, to have skin with lines for every mile you've walked, for every trip around the sun? When I watch TV, I never want to be old, they laugh at oldness on TV. But in the dark, I hold my hands up straight above me in the air like two stars and I wish for lines that prove I have been here. I wonder about Mrs. Rosen at the kitchen table, looking at the lines in her hands in the middle of the night. Who is she waiting for?

I imagine if you live in the country, you can look out your window and see the Milky Way. Anytime I want I can look out my window and see a thousand other windows, half-shaded or blaring yellow awake. I don't play outside much. I can't swim on concrete. My ears can hardly make out the rattling of the cicadas. But Mrs. Rosen says, life is with people. So maybe I can get along without cicadas.

I looked up and saw Rachel leaning back on her pillow and staring at me. Without blinking, she put out her hand to see what I wrote. I handed it to her, and she read it, her mouth in a line, her eyes moving right, then left. She didn't smile, but when she looked up at me, into my eyes, I knew she saw past the brick, to what is sparkling and moving like Lake Michigan. Good things, exciting things.

10

Orphans

$\mathcal{M}$iss Pointy likes poetry. No, she *loves* poetry. She gives us copies of poems by famous poets, one every couple of days, but she doesn't quiz us about them, so most of the kids throw them in the garbage can about two minutes after she passes them out. Miss Pointy gets mad, but she doesn't make the kids take them out of the garbage can. She says that's our bad choice, all she can do is give them to us, she can't make us take them. Darrell doesn't even look at them, he just crunches them in a ball and pretends the garbage can is a hoop, and uses the poem for a slam dunk or sometimes a three-pointer.

I never throw away the poems she gives to me. I keep them, I memorize some of them. My favorite is "Autobiographia Literaria" by Frank O'Hara.

> When I was a child
> I played by myself in a
> corner of the schoolyard
> all alone.
>
> I hated dolls and I
> hated games, animals were
> not friendly and birds
> flew away.
>
> If anyone was looking
> for me I hid behind a
> tree and cried out "I am
> an orphan."
>
> And here I am, the
> center of all beauty!
> writing these poems!
> Imagine!

Frank O'Hara called his poem "Autobiographia Literaria," which means, his life story. He told it in just a few words, not like me having to write page after page like this! I whisper these words I learned from Miss Pointy's inky ditto to keep myself company when Mom is late coming home from work. The rhythm is sweet, it reminds me of church. *The Lord is my shepherd, I shall not want. When I was a child I played by myself.* I know it is bad to say they feel the same, but I can't help it, it's true. When I'm alone opening a can of corn in the kitchen with dirty dishes piled high, I imagine coming out from behind a tree and being the center of all beauty, which doesn't seem likely, but Frank O'Hara said it happened. All he had to do was come out from behind a tree, and he was Somewhere Else. I say his words over and over again, like a spell, if I say it maybe a thousand times it will come true for me, too. Maybe the poems are a test, like Cinderella's slipper. Maybe if you can make them fit, you can be queen. That would be useful. But not everybody finds poems useful. Not everybody trusts poets, or Miss Pointy.

"Poetry is for punks," said Darrell.

"I'd like to know who isn't a punk, according to you," said Miss Pointy.

Darrell had the answer right away. "People with money."

"Then you should love poets, because they know the value of a word the way a banker knows the value of a dollar. A poem is a small economy of words. Each word is worth its weight in gold."

"Yeah, take a poem to the store, see what it buys you," sneered Darrell.

"If you spend a poem wisely, you'll get love back in return, not breakfast cereal or coffee. We're not talking food stamps here."

Raphael snorted, but it was a clumsy snort, because having a teacher talk about love is so gross you can hardly snort. Still, I wrote out my favorite poem in my best handwriting and I folded it into a little square. I didn't sign it. I tried to think who to give it to.

The door opened. It was Peaches, the Special Needs teacher. I couldn't help slinking down in my seat. She waved to me. I waved back, miserably.

"I'm here for Darrell," she said to Miss Pointy, who was writing on the chalkboard. Darrell started to get up.

"Sit down, Darrell. I didn't say you could leave

your seat," said Miss Pointy. "Where are you taking him?"

Peaches looked surprised. "Services," she said in a lowered voice.

"What services?" said Miss Pointy, not in a lowered voice. "Religious services? I wouldn't have guessed he was Jewish. He doesn't speak *any* Yiddish and his Hebrew is *entirely* illegible. But that's okay. He's a little *slow*," Miss Pointy rasped from behind her hand.

Peaches laughed. I recognized that laugh, an oh-I-heard-about-*you* laugh. "We don't like the word *slow*," said Peaches.

"We don't?" said Miss Pointy. "Then what do we do about snails and turtles and broken watches?"

Peaches straightened. "Miss Poitier, Darrell Sikes need special help. He has been *identified* as having *impulse control issues*," she said, even lower than before. "He acts out."

"Who doesn't?" Miss Pointy asked.

"No, I mean . . . haven't you checked the records?"

"Oh, wait! The records! The *records*! Oh, yes!

Darrell Sikes! You'll have to excuse me, I'm new! Ha-ha! Now let me see! I got a note about his *services* . . . just recently . . . there has been a change, now where did I put that note? Oh, I am so disorganized! Didn't you get a copy? The first week of school? About the change in Darrell's *services*? Hmmm. . . ."

Watching her, I realized I had a front-row seat to some serious and amazing lying. She wasn't looking for anything at all, she was just touching everything on her desk. First she lifted the flower vase, and then she opened a drawer; then she ran her hand over some files, and then she started rifling through a pile of papers. Then she made clicking sounds with her tongue and opened another drawer and swished her hand on the inside so you could hear all the scissors and paper clips and stapler removers clattering around. "Oh, where *is* it!"

I told myself not to jump to conclusions, but even Darrell Sikes was making a constipation face to keep from smiling. Why, why, *why*? Why would a teacher want Darrell Sikes in class, let alone *lie* to keep Darrell Sikes in class? Especially after all the trouble his psycho mother had stirred up. Especially after George Washington and his cherry tree. What happened to honesty and accountability? Why would she lie to help a crazy bad boy like Darrell Sikes? *Darrell Sikes!* It was a mystery to me.

Finally, Miss Pointy turned to Peaches and said, very decisively, "*You* must have it."

"Me! I don't remember getting any note," said Peaches. "What did it say?"

"It said, Darrell's mother has refused services this year. No pullout."

Peaches touched her lip. "You're kidding." The she lifted her arm and pointed straight at Darrell, who was pretending to be very interested in the wall. "The note said *he* is not going to be receiving services? *Him?*" She looked kind of excited, like she had been told she had won the lottery but she still couldn't quite believe it.

"Isn't it a shame?" Miss Pointy made her eyes wide. "You can call his mother. Maybe she'd be willing to talk." She smiled innocently. "Or go to the principal and tell him you lost the note. But I'm *sure* that's what the note said."

"I guess we could try it." Peaches looked worried. "I hope, though, you will come to me if you need, you know, *support*."

"That's very kind," said Miss Pointy. "I'm grateful for the offer."

Peaches brightened. "And Sahara?"

"Yes?"

"How is she . . . doing?"

"Gee, I don't know," said Miss Pointy. "Sahara! How are you doing?"

"Fine," I said in a small voice.

"Good," said Miss Pointy. "She's just fine, thanks for asking. And how is . . . your mother?"

"Fine," said Peaches. "Fine."

"Oh, that's excellent. Everybody seems to be fine."

"All right," said Peaches. "Then I'll be going."

"Fine," said Miss Pointy. "Thank you! Bye now!" She walked Peaches to the door.

Miss Pointy sat down at her desk, which she hardly ever does, and smiled behind her fingers.

She and Darrell were staring at each other. "She's a nice lady," said Miss Pointy.

"Yes, she is," said Darrell sternly. "And yet you behaved very badly."

"Uugghh," she grunted, holding her stomach. "I think I have impulse control issues." They both burst out laughing. I don't think I had ever heard Darrell laugh before. Oh, it was nice, rattling and light like a tambourine at church!

I dropped "Autobiographia Literaria" on Darrell's chair as we were heading out to recess.

"Sahara, may I see you?" Miss Pointy caught me at the classroom door. "Please stay behind. I need to speak with you for just a minute."

Speak to me about what?

She left me alone in the room while she walked the rest of the class to the exit.

I saw the pile of journals on her desk. I had been doing the journal assignments every day since I had been sick. That couldn't be it. Luz's journal was on top, stickers sparkling. I swallowed hard. I couldn't even think about if she knew how bad I was.

Did she see me drop the poem on Darrell's desk? I didn't mean anything big by it. Sometimes people just need a poem sometimes, didn't she say so? Was she going to talk to me about boys, in which case I would truly have to die? Maybe she knew I was snooping in Darrell's journal. Just once in a while, and just *Darrell's*, it's easy to find in the pile because it's all beat up and anyway you can hardly read it, the spelling is so bad. I don't even know why I would read it, it's just he is kind of surprising, it's not like he'll just come out and talk to you like a regular old boy. She said she liked snooping herself, didn't she? But I can't tell her I know that, because I was kind of snooping *then*, too, by pretending I was asleep and listening.

But what if it wasn't about Darrell at all?

Oh well, here it comes, I thought. "*Wouldn't life be easier if . . . ?*" She'll talk to me like I'm *special*. Maybe I'll have to sit out in the hall again. Maybe she read my file. Maybe . . .

Miss Pointy swept back in. "Sorry," she said.

"Miss Pointy, sometimes I look in Darrell's journal!" I exploded.

She froze for a second, and gave me a funny look. Then she unfroze. "Well, don't get caught," she said. She went right for the pile of journals, but Luz's journal was flung to the side, and so was Darrell's. She dug sloppily until she pulled out my own journal, with my name written in my tight little handwriting on the cover.

"This." She held it in the air and shook it like a lawyer on TV. "*This*."

I stood in front of Miss Pointy, but she didn't say anything more for a moment, just stood there shaking my journal. "Y . . . yes?" I squeaked.

"You'll excuse me, but I need to ask some things about *this*." Miss Pointy glared suspiciously down her pointy nose. "You're not involved in any *time-travel* debacle, are you? Like, you didn't go a few years into the future, write this, and *come back*?" She leaned forward and squinted at me in an accusing way.

"N . . . no, ma'am," I said. "I don't think so."

She took out a pair of glasses from her desk. X-ray specs, with spirals covering the lenses. "Hold still," she demanded. "Nothing personal.

Just doing my job." I nodded as though I understood. She stared into my face, hard, I think as
hard as anyone has ever looked at me besides my
own mother. I couldn't see her eyes, but her eyebrows were going up and down like she was trying
to crack a safe or defuse a bomb. "*Extraordinary!*"
she whispered. "*It's all there!*"

"What is?" I asked.

"Words," she said. "Your *talent.*" Then she pulled
something out of her tight sleeve. A gold star, with
a rainbow streaming behind it, just like the one I
had taken from Luz. "Well, that's all I needed to
know," she said. "Run along."

I burst onto the playground. Rachel and
Cordelia were waiting for me. "What did Miss
Pointy do to you?" asked Cordelia, but I ignored
her and rushed past, across the playground. To
Paris.

"What?" asked Paris. I took her hand and
slipped the sticker inside, secret-like. She looked
at her palm, and then at me. She didn't smile, and
she narrowed her eyes. But she closed her hand
around it, nodded and ran off. To Luz.

I felt myself breathe again.

I could hear feet clumsily drumming toward me as Cordelia and Rachel raced to catch up. "You in trouble?" huffed Rachel.

"No," I said. "Not anymore."

But I was wrong. When we came back in the classroom, I thought Darrell would sit on the poem I left for him and that would be that, but he saw it even though I folded it so small. He opened it, and opened it, and opened it, he didn't even sit down. Then he read it, and then his face turned a purplish color and he looked mad. He looked so mad I got scared and slunk down low in my chair.

He yelled a swear word that I know I shouldn't write, and the whole class looked at him. Then he roared, "Who put this on my chair!" as deep and loud as an angry giant. I thought about climbing into my desk, but I figured I wouldn't fit. "I ain't no orphan!" He nearly screamed. "Somebody's calling me an orphan!"

"Nobody's calling you an orphan." Miss Pointy was looking so exactly the other way of me that I knew she was thinking about me. How does she know everything? I hoped Darrell wouldn't notice. His chest heaved up and down and he looked at all of us with red, wet eyes.

I could have cried from feeling scared, and I could have cried for being so terrible, for nearly making the meanest, most special boy in school explode.

But all I could think of was how it would be at least a week before I had the chance to snoop in his journal again. And how Miss Pointy was right. Poetry is not for punks.

11

Why Teachers Get Apples

It had rained, and the fallen leaves made the sidewalk look like the floor of the kindergarten, spattered with red and yellow and green paint. Miss Pointy was telling us another story. It was about a teacher. We listened as we pressed leaves into our leaf identification books. Miss Pointy wore a crown of red maple leaves that she had stapled to some construction paper. It looked pretty against her green hair.

"She was very old."

"How old?"

"Old enough for gray hair. Old enough for a small hump in her back. Old enough for a squint in her eye." Miss Pointy squinted. "She walked to school. She got up early in the morning, so early in the morning that the dew was still on the grass."

Raphael burst out laughing. "Did she step in the *dew*?"

Miss Pointy's eyes slid, warning him. "As a matter of fact, she did, since the dew was droplets of water, Raphael. As she walked, the toes of her shoes grew wet from the *dew* and made little wet half-moons at the tips of her shoes.

"She lived out in the country, and every day she took the same route, down the brown path through the woods, across the clearing, past the play yard and to the school."

"Why didn't she drive her car?"

"It was before cars."

"My grandma's old, and she drives a car. A Buick LeSabre."

A few kids called out the makes of cars their grandmas drove. "I can wait," said Miss Pointy. And she did. "Anyway, if you ever lived in the country, you'd know why she didn't drive her car. She wanted to see the part of the day when the sun and the moon are both in the sky at the same time, on opposite ends."

"I seen that," nodded Angelina knowingly. "Uh-huh. That pretty."

"I like it, too. It reminds me of two children at opposite ends of the playground, two girls who haven't met, who are too shy to come together." I looked at Rachel and smiled. She smiled back. I felt Paris looking at me and turned around. "In the country, the air smells like snapped green beans, and the crickets are playing their legs. *Be-deep! Be-deep!*" sang Miss Pointy.

"And every time you take a step, a mess of them jump out of nowhere, uh-huh!" Angelina was getting excited. "That how it was at my grandma's house this summer. Miss Pointy telling it true."

Miss Pointy looked at Angelina while she spoke. "And isn't there something about being alone when you walk in the country, early in the morning, listening to the leaves as they whisper and twist like a hundred thousand tongues of silver-green, straining to tell a secret only to you?" We all looked up from our projects, expecting her to turn into a tree from the way her voice went soft, like a breeze. "A tree has its own language. If you knew how to listen, a tree could tell you a story for every ring in its trunk. A story about the storm whose lightning struck it in the spot where children used to climb, or about the bad-tempered squirrel who decorated its drey with diamonds that fell out of a burglar's sack, or about how the tree mourns for the old owl who was so swift and quiet, he could catch shooting stars in his claws."

"Maybe the tree was just trying to say 'Good morning,'" said Luz.

"Maybe," agreed Miss Pointy.

"Or nothing at all," said Rachel.

"Or nothing at all," repeated Miss Pointy. "Or maybe just humming. Or going over tree times tables." We groaned.

"Maybe tattling," said Janine. "Do trees tattle?"

"I expect so. Most everyone tattles at least once."

"Sakiah more than once!" Dominique called out. Everyone laughed.

"Miss Pointy! Dominique is making fun of me!" Sakiah whined.

"This is stupid. Trees don't talk or tattle or

none of that baby imagination stuff. Trees is just trees," Darrell reminded us.

"That's the spirit, Darrell. And teachers are just teachers. So this one teacher walked to school every day, past the trees, magical like Angelina's trees. . . ."

"Uh-huh!" nodded Angelina.

"Or not magical, like Darrell's trees, we really don't know," Miss Pointy confessed. "But the teacher sometimes thought they might be magic, because sometimes their knots looked like eyes and mouths and their branches looked like noses and arms, but that also could have been more baby imagination." Darrell looked smug. "She walked past these trees, into the clearing where she saw the big black crows sewing their bodies through the sky. Then, as she walked along further, she saw the farmer's horse cantering along the edge of the clearing."

I scratched *cantering* lightly onto the cover of my notebook.

"Finally she saw the schoolyard full of children."

"Sounds like a nice walk," said Janine.

Miss Pointy wrote the word *idyllic* on the board. "It was so nice and gentle and full of country charm, it was *idyllic*. But after twenty-five years of this walk, she started to get a little jealous of the things she *encountered*, or came across." I wrote these words down, too.

"What you mean, 'jealous'?"

"She would see the birds and think, 'Why can't I fly?' She would see the horse and think, 'Why can't I run?' She would see the children and think, 'Why can't I play?'"

"That's goofy," Larry remarked.

"To make matters worse, there was a boy in her class—"

"Was his name Raphael?" asked Raphael.

"Was it Dominique?" asked Dominique.

"Was it Ernie?" asked, guess who, Ernie.

"Oh, no, I can't remember his name," said Miss Pointy, with her mint-in-the-mouth smile. "I just remember he was a bad boy."

"Was his name Darrell?" asked Veronica. We laughed.

"Shut up! If he bad, that mean his teacher bad," snarled Darrell.

"You're right, Darrell!" Miss Pointy pounced. "You're exactly right! This boy was bad, but he was the same bad as his teacher, for different reasons. At home, he was beaten. He was poor. When he walked to school, the trees didn't talk to him. When he came to school, the children didn't talk to him. After some time, he started feeling jealous, too. 'Why can't I read? Why can't I write? Why can't I have friends?'" We became quiet.

"He couldn't act angry at his father, or he would beat him," Paris suggested.

"He couldn't act angry at his classmates, or they'd beat him," Kiarre added confidently, like she'd be first in line.

"So, who was left? Every day, he'd be angry at his teacher. It was old times. She could have beaten him. Those were the days!" Miss Pointy sighed. "But in twenty-five years, she hadn't beaten a child. She didn't want to beat him."

"She had to love him," said Rashonda. "Teachers are paid to love children."

"Teachers aren't paid much, so they don't love us much," said Larry. Miss Pointy stared at Larry, surprised. "Most don't love us much," he corrected himself.

"That's silly, Larry. Teachers aren't paid to love children. You can't legally pay someone to love you," Miss Pointy explained. "Loving children is what teachers do for extra credit. It's not the main assignment."

"Seems to me that the extra credit is more important than the main assignment," observed Cordelia.

"You're right, smart Cordelia," said Miss Pointy, taking out the Happy Box. Cordelia looked surprised, and took a long time to choose a star. "Extra credit is done of your own free will. Work and love given out of free will is always more joyous, better-quality stuff."

Raphael gagged. "Quit talking about love! Get back to the boy who got beat."

"Okay. So there's this boy and this teacher, neither of them working for extra credit. The boy being as mad and mean as he can to the

131

teacher. Puts a tack in her seat, chalk in her eraser."

"Old-fashion mess," grumbled Darrell.

"And the worst part is, he talks back. Talks back like crazy. He won't do a thing the teacher says. He stands up on his desk and beats his chest and shouts."

"Like King Kong!" breathed Ernie.

Darrell stood on his chair and demonstrated.

"Thank you, Darrell. Like that. Well. The teacher doesn't know what to do. Every morning she walks to school, she thinks so hard about this bad boy, she doesn't see the moon or the sun or hear the trees talking. Her mind is so full of the hard day ahead."

"Girlfriend needs the trouble basket," observed Kiarre.

"Uh-huh." Janine and Kiarre slapped hands.

"She sees the birds and the horse and the children, and her heart starts to crack. Things that made her happy as a younger person were the very things that made her sad as the days wore on.

"Every day, the boy wouldn't do his work.

Every day she felt the lashes of the boy's words, like a whip against all her years of service."

"She should beat his ass!" Rashonda exploded.

"School language," reminded Miss Pointy. "Rashonda, do you think that would really work?"

"Nah. But she'd feel better."

"Yeah! Make her beat his ass in the story!" urged Raphael, also forgetting school language.

"Yeah, he beating *her*, you said so! 'Words like a whip!'"

"Make her whip him back!"

"Let's vote! Who says, 'Whip his ass?'"

"We are not voting," said Miss Pointy, her arms crossed like she does when she's waiting. "Stories are not a democracy. Thank God." Finally, we quieted down.

"I'm disappointed in you," she said finally. "She didn't beat him. I told you. She hadn't beaten anyone in twenty-five years, and she wasn't going to give this boy the satisfaction of breaking her record."

"You go, girl!" whispered Kiarre.

"One day, she gave the children an

assignment. 'What I wish.' They had to write in their journals."

"They had journals back then?"

"She was ahead of her time. After she gave the assignment, she realized she gave it because she wished someone would give it to her." *Like when I ask Rachel a question*, I thought. "The teacher took out a blank piece of paper. The teacher wrote simply, 'I wish I were a bird. I wish I were a horse. I wish I were a child.'"

"Three wishes. She greedy," said Leon.

"She should of wished that boy out of her school," grunted Tanaeja.

"Well, at that very same time, the boy wrote his wish down. He wrote, simply, 'I wish she was not a teacher at this school.'"

"Why he write that? He could have written anything. He could have wished for a million dollars."

"He wrote that because he knew his teacher would read it. He knew it would hurt her. He wanted to hurt somebody, because it felt like somebody was always hurting him.

"That afternoon, at the end of the day, the teacher collected the papers, took her bag of books and left the school, walking back past the schoolyard, the clearing, and into the woods.

"The next day, when the boy came to school, his teacher wasn't there. There was a substitute. He felt a little scared."

"What for?" asked Cordelia. "It was just a wish."

"Then he felt so sorry and wished her back and they lived happily ever after, and all the trees sang and danced, tra-la," said Darrell.

"If you think you've got a better ending than I have . . ." Miss Pointy said, sighing.

"Be quiet, Darrell," warned Dominique.

"The replacement was mean. He beat the children, he beat the boy, too, first time he opened his mouth. This new teacher would have none of that. The children didn't defend the boy, they were tired of the way he acted in class and were glad he was being controlled. The new teacher saw the boy couldn't do much, and he didn't call on him. It was nice at first, but then the boy started to feel invisible and empty. He worried that it was his wish that made this happen. But he had nobody to ask about it, no one to assure him that his fears were silly.

"One morning he was walking along the path, and he heard something that he had never heard before. It seemed to him that the trees were talking, in a language he had heard all his life yet never had come to understand. He stood still, between the school and home. Frightened, he ran off the path, and when he stopped running, he saw an apple tree. This cheered him up, and he forgot his fear. He pulled some fruit from the tree, and ate on the way to school, the hungry knot in his stomach unwinding slowly.

"When he arrived at school he was so satisfied that he skewered his last apple on the fence post.

"Out the window, he could see the apple being visited through the day by a little bird. He watched as the bird flew in wide circles, around and around the school, alighting now and then on the apple to eat and sing. The boy felt another knot unwind within him.

"Time passed. Every day, he picked apples

from the tree and stuck one on the post for the bird. One day, he decided to see if there were any other trees in the woods. That's when he found his old teacher's bag, sprawled on the ground, and under his teacher's damp books was the last assignment he had done for her. Reminded of his terrible wish, he wondered if wishing it had made it so. But he only wondered for a moment, because he was older."

"Had more sense," said Larry.

"Did he? Well, he took the books and dried them out. Every day after school, he studied them on his own."

"Why'd he do *that*?" Raphael laughed.

"It beat going home," said Darrell. I looked at him, maybe everybody did. Miss Pointy, too.

"Now a horse started visiting the post where the boy put his apple. He'd gnaw it off in a bite or two, and then gallop around the clearing. Can you imagine how nice it was for the boy, watching that beautiful, free creature?

"More time passed. Do you know what happens when time passes?"

"People get old," said Sakiah.

"People die," said Rachel.

"Both those things happened. The boy got older. His father died, and the mean teacher retired and moved away. So the superintendent came in, the boss of the schools. He drilled the class with review problems. The boy who had been so bad shone like a star. The superintendent asked if he would like to teach at the little school when he graduated that spring. He said yes.

"When the leaves began to fall," Miss Pointy said, picking up some dried leaves from her desk and letting them somersault on to the floor, "the doors of the schoolhouse were open, and behind the desk sat a young man with the start of a beard and a mind full of knowledge. No one could have guessed that he was once a hungry little boy who stood on his chair and thumped his chest and was beaten with a strap by his father, no one could have guessed that he had wished his teacher away, or that for all that evilness and sadness, he still remembered to stab an apple on the post every day for his bird and his horse.

"He stood at the door and rang the bell, and the children who were playing in the yard came running to the door and filed inside. In came a little girl with brown hair pulled tight, and freckles and sunburn and a smile so wide you would think her pigtails were stretching her face."

"The third wish!" gasped Angelina.

Miss Pointy smiled. "The little girl had in her hand a big red apple. She handed it to the man.

"'What's this for?' he asked the girl.

"'This is for all the days when I was a bird, and all the days I was a horse. You gave me an apple every day, and now I will give an apple to you.'" Miss Pointy took the apple off of her own desk and put it on Darrell's desk. Darrell just watched her face, and pretended not to notice the apple.

"Every day the little girl gave her teacher an apple, paying back the small favors of his boyhood. The other children saw this and thought she was trying to be the favorite, and they started giving the teacher apples, too. But in his heart, the little girl who had once been his teacher was indeed his favorite. And as the days wore on, there was no little girl happier to be a little girl and no grown-up happier to be a grown-up than the two at that school, and their satisfaction was such that there was never a need for another wish. The end."

"What kind of story is that?" asked Darrell.

"I made it up," said Miss Pointy. "From a dream I had. You like it?"

"It's not a real story if you just made it up, is it?" wondered Leon.

Yes, it is, I thought. *It will be real as soon as I write it down. It will be a real story about a girl who wished it were real.*

"I like it," said Sakiah.

"You would," said Darrell.

"It's a fairy tale," said Angelina.

"Ain't no fairies, or royalty," said Veronica.

"It's a *pourquoi* tale," said Paris. We had learned that *pourquoi* means "why" in French, and *pourquoi* tales explain why things happen. "It tells why teachers get apples."

"Maybe you're both right," said Miss Pointy.

"Maybe they're both wrong," said Sakiah. "Sounds to me like a fable."

"A fable's got to have a moral at the end," Ernie reminded her. Sakiah wrinkled her nose and stuck out her tongue.

"So if this is a fable, what's the moral? The lesson?" asked Miss Pointy.

We were quiet, thinking, and watching other kids think.

"What goes around comes around," blurted Larry.

"Tit for tat," snorted Raphael. Dominique snorted, too.

Miss Pointy ignored them. "Hmmm, I don't know, Larry. Try to put the moral into your own words, not a cliché, something people have said before."

We thought some more. "Wishes come true," said Luz.

"Good try," said Miss Pointy, "but I don't know if that's a lesson that is always so. What else can we come up with?"

"Wishes are powerful," said Dominique.

"Good," said Miss Pointy.

"Things change. They don't always stay the

same," said Cordelia. "Like, you don't have to stay a kid."

"That's a good one, too. Anyone else?"

"School is a powerful place where things change and wishes come true," Paris said slowly. "It's a place where you can grow up, if you let yourself." It sounded like a kiss-up answer. It also sounded right.

Miss Pointy took out her Happy Box. We all looked on jealously as Paris chose a sticker. "Anyone else?" We all looked at each other. Paris's answer seemed good enough; it got the Happy Box, didn't it? "What's the lesson?" Miss Pointy insisted. We were all quiet. My wrist twitched, and I started to raise my hand.

The bell rang.

"Oh-oh," said Miss Pointy. "Put away your leaf books and let's go."

"You spent all that time telling us a story," accused Cordelia.

"Do you want me to apologize?" asked Miss Pointy. "Fine. I'm sorry we didn't have time for our journals today. Write in them tonight, if you like.

What *you* would wish for." We stood up and gathered our things. I imagined what everyone would write:

> I want a castle of stickers
> with a special sticker room, no,
> a hundred rooms all filled with
> stickers and a real unicorn
> that I could ride . . .

> **I wish I was invisible so I**
> **could walk home without anybody**
> **bothering me . . .**

> I wish I didn't have to watch the
> baby after school, I never get to go
> out . . .

> *I wish for a robot that looks just*
> *like me who would take my tests . . .*

> I wish I was a superstar in the WNBA . . .

My file, I thought.

I wish for the letters in my file.

Miss Pointy yelled over the scraping and clonking sound of us turning chairs upside down, putting them on our desks, and the noise seemed to wake me up from my daydream. That's a silly wish, I thought. Of all the wishes! Wish for a million dollars. Wish to look in Miss Pointy's closet and get to choose any dress I want. Wish Daddy would come home. Wish for something silly like that. . . .

Quick, I wrote a P with a line through it over what I had scribbled.

Miss Pointy stood at the door and said goodbye to each of us. Rachel stayed behind and started making her watery stripes across the board with the sponge.

Miss Pointy grabbed me by my jacket hood. I hung behind. "I saw your hand. So what do you think that story was about?"

"Paris said it."

"Really?" Miss Pointy leaned against the

threshold and crossed her arms. "Stories mean different things to different people."

Should I tell her? I looked at the floor. She waited. I waited, too, but I *wanted* to tell her. "People thought that boy was one way, but . . . inside each person, I think there's a secret person," I said.

"Huh," she said. "That's interesting. Do you have a secret person inside of you?"

"No . . ."

"Yes she does," announced Rachel, from across the room, not looking up from her chore.

"Yes," I corrected myself. I could not look at Miss Pointy. "But only you know my secret. You and Rachel." Rachel kept on wiping the board, but she had that same mint-in-the-mouth expression that Miss Pointy wears.

And there was Miss Pointy, wearing it too. "I don't know if that's true," she said. "Secret people are hard to keep inside. Especially if they are wonderful. You, for instance, are leaking." I looked up, feeling shy. She was smiling, but her eyes were serious.

When I left the room, the hall was empty, but Paris and Luz were leaning against some lockers. They looked up when they saw me. They cast long shadows in the afternoon light that came through the exit. *They're going to beat me up*, I thought. *They're skinny, but there's two of them. If they're wearing rings, I'm done for.* I walked and could hear my footsteps clicking.

"Hi," I said as bravely as I could.

"Hi," said Paris. She looked nervously at Luz, who looked nervously back at her and stuck her thumbs in the straps of her backpack. *Well, this is a very polite way to start a fight*, I thought. *Oh, my God. I'm going to get beat up by the nicest girls in school.*

"We were wondering," Paris said. "We're thinking of starting a club."

Oh?

"For people who like books," she went on.

"And esteekers," added Luz. "Do you like esteekers?"

I looked at Paris, who pursed her lips. "I guess," I said.

"And I know you like books. So we were wondering if you'd like to be in it," said Paris.

"Who else is in it?"

"Just us," said Luz.

"For now," said Paris, then added quickly, "but anyone who wants to join can, though, right Luz? We don't like to leave people out." Luz seemed to both nod her head yes and shake her head no at the same time, in total agreement. It was contagious. I shook like a bobble-head.

"When's the first meeting?" I asked.

"I don't know," said Paris. "Let's talk about it while we walk home. We go your way. Can you be at the library this Saturday?"

"Sure," I said. "You know what? My mom works at a restaurant, and after the meeting we can go there and eat all the pancakes we want for free."

"Wow!" they said.

Yeah, wow! I thought, as we walked out the door together.

<u>My wish by Darrell Sikes</u>

Ok ok I am a orfin! I wish for
a friend.

    a. You are not an orphan, you live
       with your mother and

    b. You already have a friend.

    a. your not supos to look wen I write
       p at the top and
    b. dont gimme that teecher mess

    a. Sometimes I snoop and
    b. I'm not your friend, I'm your
       ally.

    a. My moms not my frend shes my mom
and

    b. I dont have anthin to write for Let-
ter b

    a. You've got a friend in this

classroom right now and you
don't even know it. Why don't
you keep your eyes peeled?

b. I also don't have anything to
write for letter b.

c. Wait, I just thought of a b. See
me, I need to help you with your
punctuation.

How is it Im posed to keep my eyes
peeled
No id never be able to peel my eyes
and look for a frend oh no no no cant be
helped so wood you mine peeling my eyes
for me sins you are kine enugh to show
consern in that ragard

HAHA

12

Name-calling

"I think I've told you enough stories to choke a horse," Miss Pointy said, surprising us the next afternoon. "I'm in the mood to do some listening. Remember I suggested a while back that you could write stories in your journal about how you got your name? I was thinking that maybe some of you wouldn't mind reading those aloud."

This was very exciting, because, of course, we were not allowed to read other people's journals without their permission (even though I had snuck again and read Darrell's the other afternoon). Miss Pointy passed them out. Several kids waved their hands in the air. "Pick me!" "Pick me!" In my imagination, I raised my hand, but then in my imagination, she called on me and I had to read it, and kids yawned and threw paper at me. So instead of raising my hand, I slunk down in my seat and smiled at my classmates. I was eager to hear what they had written.

"Ernie? You have your hand raised so quietly." Boys who weren't called on groaned. "Come, stand in front of my desk so we all can hear you."

"My full name is Ernest Meija the Second," he read, "and I was named after Ernest Meija the First, my mother's brother. He is a fireman with the Chicago Fire Department. He was the first child born in this country from my family. He helps my family a lot. He has never been killed on the job, but he had a friend who was. He told me when he is fighting fires he always tries to save the family pet if he can. I think he is very brave and I am proud to be named after my brave uncle Ernie."

He looked up, finished.

"Comments?" asked Miss Pointy.

"Your uncle Ernie sounds cute," said Mariah.

"Yeah," agreed Janine and Cordelia.

"How old is your uncle Ernie, Ernie?" asked Miss Pointy.

"He's around thirty, I think."

"Too old for you, girls," said Miss Pointy. "And hundreds of years too young for me."

"How old *are* you?" asked Sakiah.

"In human years, or teacher years?" Miss Pointy answered, and then quickly called on someone else.

"That's nice, he saves cats," said Larry.

"Ees good," said Boris, who hardly ever talks. He was smiling openly at Ernie, his friend. He looked like a proud poppa. Ernie blushed.

Miss Pointy looked pleased. "Well done, Ernie!" Some thin applause. "Who else here has been named after a family member?" Many hands went up. "It's nice to have a family name with some history. Paris? Your name has some history, too. Why don't you step right up."

Paris cleared her throat.

"'My Name,' by Paris McCray. My mother and father named me after the capital of France, the city of love and romance. For instance, in France they love pancakes called *crêpes*. I know how to make them, my mom showed me. They love poodles so much that they let them eat in the restaurants like people. There is an Eiffel Tower there, and many great churches, and many artists went to live there, including but not limited to the great Josephine Baker, who danced naked before it was in style to do so."

"Woo!" said Raphael. "I see London, I see France!"

"It is all very exotic," Paris continued, "and furthermore people speak French all the time, for example. I do not know how to speak French, but I hope to learn in high school. My mom and dad never went to France. They were going to go, but then my mom got pregnant. It was a surprise because my parents already had four kids. They needed the money more than the trip, so my mom said if we can't go to Paris, then Paris will come to us. Someday I will go to Paris and wave from the top of the Eiffel Tower to my parents who will be eating crêpes down below. The end."

"That was good," said Veronica.

Cordelia disagreed, and showed it by gagging. "Naked people! Dogs in restaurants! Paris sounds like a filth hole!"

"Oh, Cordelia, be quiet," said Tanaeja. "You don't even know what you're talking about."

Cordelia jutted out her chin. "Excuse me! I have been to France, and speak fluent French!"

This was, of course, the wrong thing to say in front of someone named Poitier. "*Est-ce que c'est vrai? As-tu mangé un croque-monsieur quand tu as visité? Moi, j'adore les croques-monsieurs, presque plus que les crêpes.*"

"I'm sorry." Cordelia sniffed. "I'm afraid I only speak *northern* French."

"*Naturellement*," Miss Pointy said innocently. "I was merely wondering how you found the grilled cheeses over there."

"I found them extremely filthy," said Cordelia.

"Really! I found them delicious. I also found your paragraph delicious, Paris. Very romantic. *Vive la France!*" We applauded especially loudly, just to spite Cordelia.

"*Vive la* Paris McCrepe!" cheered Dominique. Paris bowed elegantly.

"I wish I had me a plane ticket to France," said Kiarre.

"Would you like to go, too, Kiarre?" asked Miss Pointy.

"No. I'd just love to send Cordelia and get her lying self out of this classroom."

We laughed. "Now, now," said Miss Pointy, "kind words in the classroom." She didn't say Cordelia wasn't a liar. And Kiarre said sorry, but she said it more to Miss Pointy than to Cordelia. I felt a little sorry for Cordelia. Just a little.

"Paris wasn't the only one who was named after a place. Sahara? Would you read what you wrote?"

Me? I hadn't been up in front of a class in at least a year. Or two years. Didn't she know that about me? Suddenly, I wished she were the kind of teacher who looked at records.

"Sahara?"

There it was again, she was calling my name. I tried to feel my legs. They felt like two Popsicle sticks with all the Popsicle melted off. I shook my head, no.

"Oh, come on, Sahara," said Miss Pointy.

"Please?" coaxed Paris.

I looked at Rachel. She smiled, and nodded her head, excited.

"I'll go, then," Cordelia sighed, like she was being inconvenienced. "'Cordelia Carbuncle: Ruby of the Seven Seas.'"

"Sahara, just get up and read your damn thing!" Kiarre barked. I teetered forward.

I stared down at my journal entry. I felt all eyes on me, I felt the room tilt just slightly. "I didn't check the spelling," I confessed.

Miss Pointy shrugged. "Neither here nor there."

"It's personal," I whispered hoarsely.

"All good writing is personal," she whispered hoarsely back. "Pretend you're reading somebody else's writing, you'll get through it."

"It's weird," I pleaded. "It's long."

"Not as weird and long as waiting for you to do this," said Miss Pointy, not whispering. Embarrassed, I turned to face the class. "Take a deep breath," she suggested, behind me. I did.

"'My Name,' by Sahara Jones," I began.

"Louder," she ordered.

"'My Name', by Sahara Jones," I said again.

"Louder, and with expression!"

I swallowed. "'MY NAAAAME', by SaHAra JONES!" I yelled. The class laughed.

"Good," said Miss Pointy. "Go on."

I can see how my daddy thought my name was a good idea at the time I was born. He must have thought that naming me after the biggest part of Africa would make me special. But special wears off. At least, it did for my daddy. He left me and my mom when I was in the third grade. We're not sure where he is.

When he left, Mom changed our last name back to Jones, which was her name before she got married. "You can change your first name, too, if you want," she told me. "We don't need nothing that man gave us."

That last line wasn't so hard to write. Why was it so hard to read? I swallowed again.

"Go on," said Miss Pointy. "You're doing great."

I didn't mind my name, and I didn't exactly agree with my mom, but I didn't let on. It's not every day that your mother gives you permission to change your name.

"Okay," I said. "Call me Shaquana."

"Shaquana!" My mom wrinkled her nose.

I heard the class laugh. It startled me. I found my place again and kept reading.

"Jennifer?"

"Girl, I know you're joking," Mom said. "Put a little more thought into it than that. A name's got to last a long time."

I ran through lots of names in my mind for a few days. Aisha. Candace. Saundra. Camille. Shalonda. Dolores. Denise. It made my head spin.

One day we had a substitute, and during science she showed us a video about the great African desert, the Sahara. A few kids laughed and pointed out that I was named after a desert, but once that was said, nobody seemed very interested in the video. Except for me. I was finally going to see what my father named me after.

The sand had ripples all through it, like it was remembering water. A sun dipped down at the edge of the horizon. It shook in the waves of heat like a great orange fist. The desert beneath spread flat and dry, knowing that under its sands lived scorpions that are especially venomous, snakes that can smell the taste of you, tortoises that know no time. The desert is mystery. To cross it, you have to be a camel. You have to use what you have for yourself, keep what you need inside yourself, in a big sagging hump. A camel only spares enough to spit. This is the way to survive the desert, I thought, as they showed the darkness of night leaning over the dunes.

As the video played I could hear the winds picking up as the desert night grew colder and colder. I felt my own teeth chatter, and I couldn't stop them. I wasn't Sahara, the girl, anymore. I was Sahara, the desert, filled with secret scorpions. And even though I know that deserts are very dry places, I started to cry and cry and cry.

I guess somebody told the teacher, because the next thing I knew, she was kneeling next to my desk saying, "What's the matter, honey?"

And I told her, "I think I'm having a heart attack."

She looked back at me like maybe she was going to

have one, too. She made me open my mouth and say "Ahhh," like you can tell if someone is having a heart attack by looking down her throat. She pulled me out of my seat and dragged me down the hall to the office. But as soon as I was out of that classroom and away from that movie, I felt better right away.

"My name is Sahara," I said to my mom, first thing when I came through the door. "Sahara Jones."

She looked at me in such a way, I wondered if she was swallowing a pill.

Finally, she said, "Wish I'd-a thought of it first."

But my name has changed since my daddy left. I didn't change it, and neither did my mom. Last year when I was in Special Needs, some kids started calling me Sahara Special. I know they were saying it to be mean, but now I like it anyway. My names are given to me, but they are also names that I choose to take. And the choosing makes all the difference.

"I stopped writing there because the bell started ringing. Plus, I was finished anyway," I said. There was silence. "So, the end." There was still silence.

My leg was shaking so hard, I felt like I wanted to hold on to it with both hands. My palms were sweating, and my heart was pounding. I could not bring myself to lift my eyes from my journal. There was no noise. Were they still in the room? Were they all asleep? Were they still *alive*?

"Comments?" said Miss Pointy.

Still nothing. Out of the corner of my eye, I saw Darrell give me a funny look.

"Come on," urged Miss Pointy. "Let's give her some feedback."

"Well, what you want us to say?" Angelina finally said.

"Actually, I have some notes here," Cordelia cleared her throat. "I think she meant to say, 'I was finally going to see that after which I was named,' not 'I was finally going to see what I was named after.'"

Michael's voice even rolled its eyes. "What's the difference?"

"The difference is English," said Cordelia.

"She speaks English. There's plenty big words,"

said Janine. "How'd she know all those words like
. . . what'd you say?"

"Darkness of night leaning over the duuuuu-
unnnnessss," hummed Angelina. "Tortoisessssss that
know no tiiiiimmmmmmme."

"Yeah, like that! How'd she know all those
words like that!"

"Yeah, she writes like a grown-up!" said
Raphael. "All that 'he said, she said.'"

"I read a lot," I mumbled. See, they hated it!
They thought it was weird! They thought I was
weird! I *was* weird! I blinked; I would not cry in
front of them.

"Maybe she copied it from somewhere," said
Leon.

"No, she didn't," came Rachel's voice. I was surprised to hear it. "She told me this summer that
she was going to be a writer, and she is going to
write a book."

"A real book? In the library?" Ernie was
impressed.

"Uh-huh," I said. Luz leaned over and whispered something to Paris, and they both looked at

me, excited. I bet they were planning the next meeting of our club, for people who like reading *and* writing. And . . . uh . . . esteekers.

"What's it going to be about?" asked Sakiah.

"No, no, no!" Miss Pointy stood up. "Don't ask writers what they're writing about. If it comes out of their mouths, it won't come out of their pens."

"At first, I thought it was funny. Then it wasn't funny at all," said Ameer.

"It was *great*!" yelled Paris. I looked up.

"You got a good imagination," said Rashonda.

"Girl-I-di-int-know-that-you-could-write-like-that!" rapped Tanaeja. "Sahara-how-your-journal-get-down-like-that!"

The class laughed. I would have laughed, too, if I hadn't been so terrified.

"Sorry I said you copied," Leon said. "I just . . . it was good, Sahara."

"Yeah, Sahara," said Sakiah. "*Wow*."

"I theenk Sahara should get an esteeker," said Luz.

"She did," said Miss Pointy. "It's on her journal."

"I thought it was long," said Raphael. Everyone

ignored him, except for Tanaeja. "Course you did," she cooed, and patted his hand. He snarled at her and pulled his hand away.

"Well, what's the point of Sahara's story?" Everyone settled down and looked at one another. "Ernie? You're good at morals. What do you think the moral of the story is?" Ernie shook his head. "Anyone?"

"Don't judge book by its cover," came a voice.

"Who said that?" Miss Pointy looked around. "*Darrell!* I'm so proud of you!" She grinned so that all her teeth showed, and Darrell smiled back the same way, mimicking her.

"Yay, Darrell!" said Raphael.

"Don't make a stink about it," said Darrell.

"Yay, Sahara Special, then!" said Mariah.

"Yeah, yay, Sahara!" said Tanaeja and Kiarre.

I looked red-faced to Rachel, who was nodding and back to her quiet self . . . but this time I didn't mind, not one bit.

The whole class cheered. They cheered so loudly, I couldn't hear my heart breaking. But I could feel it. I guess Miss Pointy could see it. "And for such inspirational writing, Sahara can be messenger and deliver this note for me. And Cordelia, you waited so patiently. It's your turn."

The class groaned, more jealous about my messenger job than they were about my writing. "As I was saying," Cordelia started up. "'Cordelia Carbuncle: Ruby of the Seven Seas.'"

I took the envelope and stepped quickly out in the hall. I wiped my eyes on my sleeve and leaned against the wall. Then I looked down at the envelope, expecting to see OFFICE, or a room number. It said SAHARA.

I opened it.

The note said, *Turn left*. So I turned left.

The note said, *Walk three paces*. So I took three steps.

The note said, *Turn left again*. So I did, and I was facing an old locker.

We weren't allowed to keep things in lockers because the upper-grade kids kept stealing lunches from them. So the lockers were used as storage for old textbooks. The note said, *Open*. So I opened the locker.

There was a small cactus in a pot, with a beautiful red flower in bloom at the top.

And behind it, a brown folder with my name on it.

My file.

The classroom door opened. Out stepped Darrell, holding the boys' pass. He closed the door, and faced me straight on, head bent, eyebrows bent, frowning.

"What?" I squirmed.

"You sent me that dumb poem, didn't you." I was too embarrassed to deny it. "I am *not* an orphan," he said.

"I know." I squirmed some more.

"And," he said, "neither are you."

He walked away, whistling, toward the boys' room. I reached behind the cactus and pulled out my file. I clutched it to my chest with both arms.

13

Autobiographia Literaria

I ran into my room at home and closed the door. I couldn't wait.

I spilled the envelope out on to my bed. On the top was a page ripped out of my journal that I had forgotten about.

Do teachers have secrets?

Yes. For instance, I like to give kids presents sometimes on the sly if I know what they really want. That's a good secret. Teachers' bad secrets, like getting caught smoking in the custodian's office or being fresh to the principal or having boyfriends that ride motorcycles, are kept in a dreadful file

*somewhere. It's hard to get to a
teacher's file. But student files are so
easy to get your hands on.*

Next in the pile was a letter from my mom. "I request my daughter be removed from the special education program." I smiled and turned the letter over.

And then, there were the letters I had written.

Dear Daddy, I miss you. . . .

Dear Daddy, When are you coming home. . . .

Dear Daddy, Why didn't you take me with you. . . .

Dear Daddy, It was my birthday, I wished it on my candles that you would call, and you didn't. . . .

Dear Daddy, Mom says you don't help with anything anymore but I don't care, I know you'll come back and help us. . . .

Dear Daddy, There's a hole in my heart. . . .

I turned them over, one by one, like cards in a fortune-teller's deck. But these weren't telling me the future, these were telling me the past. It was sad to see them, but it was funny, too, that they had kept them. Even though as I leafed through them I realized they all said the same thing, they all told the same story.

Miss Pointy says, the main character is the one who changes.

I held one of the letters I had written in third grade up to the light from the window. I couldn't help smiling at my round, careful cursive. *Dear Daddy, Can't you see from my handwriting what kind of girl I am, will that make it enough for you to come home to me?*

The clouds outside were high and generous big, moving fast. I opened the window. I closed my eyes and held out the piece of paper, let it flutter in my open palms. When I opened my eyes, I saw it flapping in the sky like a bird, flying away.

I tossed out the next letter, and the next, making birds, until the last one. As I watched them tumble past the brown brick of the buildings, east,

east to the lake, I wrote one last letter in my mind's eye.

> Dear Daddy,
>   I love you. I miss you. I hope someday you're smart enough to be sorry, but if you're not, that's okay. I'm smart enough not to keep all this in my file.
>   Love, your daughter and secret writer,
>   Sahara Jones, now and forever

In my mind's eye, I ripped it in half. In my mind's eye, I let the pieces loose, let them climb the stairway of the wind past the buildings, past the lake, past the moon and stars and sun, to Somewhere Else, the place where my father now lives.

And then, I pulled out my notebook and wrote, and wrote, and wrote. Not about my *Heart-Wrenching Life Story*, but all these pages about a teacher and her *Amazing Adventures* with her class, all about a teacher's file and a teacher's secrets. I wrote about friends and tattletales, bravery and fear, but for the first time, it didn't all have to be straight true, I could write about all the exciting things I wished were true. The words moved like wheels across the paper. I didn't count pages or minutes. Mom tapped on my door, and only then did I notice the sun had gone down and I was writing nearly in the dark. The whole apartment was warm. The radiators clanged like music. I could smell meat loaf in the oven. Mom had fried potatoes with lots of onions and butter. She was making my favorite meal for dinner. Where had I been?

"You've been sitting in here forever." My mother flicked on the light switch and squinted at me. Had I? It was like magic, like Rip Van Winkle, who fell asleep and found himself a hundred years older when he opened his eyes. I unfurled my fingers, fossilized and aching around the pen.

"Dinner's on."

"Almost finished."

"Whatcha writing now?" she asked.

"Sketching out some adventures," I confessed. "I've already finished my *Autobiographia Literaria*." In one second I was embarrassed that I was so eager. Mom's eyes were laughing at me.

"Who, now?"

"My life story. I have had a very interesting life," I said, defending myself.

"Me, too." Her eyes were glinting. "Fascinating. And it's over?"

I ignored her. "I'm starting something new."

"Maybe you'll show it to me sometime?"

"If you want," I said. "It'll be in the library." I felt her bristle. Did she think I was being fresh? I turned in my chair to correct myself, to explain that it *was* promised to the library, behind section 940, to be found by someone in the future, someone whose life will be made more exciting just by reading my *Heart-Wrenching Life Story and Amazing Adventures*. But the doorway was already empty.

While we ate, I could hear the silverware against the plates.

"It's good, Mom," I complimented her and smiled. She smiled back. She looked at me for a long time. It made me nervous, so I looked at my meat loaf.

"So, what did you do at school?"

I shrugged. "Kids read aloud from their journals."

"Lord, they sure waste your time at school, don't they?" said Mom. "Just writing and talking about any old thing that pops into your head. Bet them kids in the suburbs learning calculus by now." She didn't know what to say next, I could tell. "You're growing up," is what she finally came out with.

"How do you know?" I teased.

"You're not talking to me." She smiled sadly.

"I talk to you," I filled my mouth with potatoes.

"I guess I don't know how to speak your language."

I laughed a little, like she had made a joke, like we were talking about why firemen wear red suspenders or what time it is when an elephant sits on a fence, and she laughed, too. We ate the rest of the meal in thoughtful silence.

But that night, I climbed into bed with her, and she didn't say anything against it. She held me firm with one arm around my shoulder, like she didn't want me to go anywhere. I stared at the ceiling and felt uneasy and excited at once, like I was destined to end up Somewhere Else anyway, no matter how she held me.

"Sing to me," she said, half-joking. "Tell me a story. Tell me your autobiographia whatever."

I took a breath. I thought about what poem to spend. I spoke to her softly, like I was singing a lullaby.

```
When I was a child
I played by myself in a
corner of the schoolyard
all alone.

I hated dolls and I
hated games, animals were
not friendly and birds
flew away.

If anyone was looking
for me I hid behind a
tree and cried out "I am
an orphan."

And here I am, the
```

```
center of all beauty!
writing these poems!
Imagine!
```

Imagine, I thought.

She gently stroked my hair, making sure I was there. It was comforting, but now, I didn't need it. It was extra credit.

ESMÉ RAJI CODELL

is an avid collector of sparkly stickers and a pretty good roller skater. She is also the author of *Educating Esmé: Diary of a Teacher's First Year*, which won an Alex Award, given for the best adult books for young adults. She has worked as a children's bookseller, teacher, and school librarian, and now runs the popular children's literature Web site www.planetesme.com. Esmé lives in Chicago with her husband and son.

This
Book
is

Kathryn
Pratt

from
Mrs.
Hale

TOMÁS TAKES CHARGE

TOMÁS
TAKES
CHARGE
SEQUOYAH SCHOOL

by CHARLENE JOY TALBOT

Illustrated by Reisie Lonette

ᖇᘿᑕ®

LIBRARY EDITION 1970
RESPONSIVE ENVIRONMENTS CORP.
Englewood Cliffs, N.J. 07632
LOTHROP, LEE & SHEPARD CO., INC.

NEW YORK

To Miss Carmie Wolfe,
who encouraged me in high school

Four lines from PEGGY O'NEIL
by Harry Pease, Ed. G. Nelson and
Gilbert Dodge
Copyright 1921/Copyright Renewal 1949,
Leo Feist Inc., New York, N.Y.
Used by permission.

Second printing, October 1967

CONTENTS

1

MRS. MALLOY TAKES A STAND

Tomás Lorca stood in the open end of a wooden packing crate. He closed his eyes. I will count to twenty-five, he told himself. When I look, Papa will be coming. With a bag of food. No, two bags, one in each arm.

He counted, then looked. One way and the other. Except for a truck in the next block, the street was empty. Friday-night empty. From Friday night until Sunday evening, the bare loading docks along Greenwich Street, the huge locked doors, the vacant windows of the warehouses belonged to Tomás—Tomás and the twenty or so other people who lived in Washington Market.

The rest of the week, day and night, the trucks were there. They rumbled over the cobblestones, waited patiently in line until they could move ahead or back up across the sidewalks to the loading docks of the warehouse.

Tomás leaned against the rough, new-smelling boards of the crate and closed his eyes again. This time he would count to fifty. His thick hair was dusty black; his face, pale, except for the brown-purple shadows under his closed eyes. The shadows were from hunger, a hunger which had been growing for days until now he was seeing the barbecued chicken again, sizzling and browning inside a glass case. These days he always saw it inside the glass case.

Tomás was eleven and beginning to grow. The old red-striped T-shirt was too short. So were last year's suit pants, but his rubber-thong sandals, found in a trash can, fitted just right.

A summer evening breeze wandered up Greenwich Street from the Battery. It brought the smell of salt water. Even the smells changed on Friday night; no more whiffs of cinnamon or of roasting coffee until Monday morning.

He opened his eyes again at the count of fifty. A Market worker went shuffling around the corner of the building where the coffee was roasted. Nobody else.

Tomás climbed to the top of his crate and watched old Mrs. Stefano come out from the hot apartment house. She lived on the fifth floor. He watched her cross the street and sit on a loading dock.

A cruising patrol car passed, and then the Market watchman, driving his blue car.

The evening was cool for the first of July—in fact perfect. Soon the street lights came on. Tomás jumped to the sidewalk, gave the crate a farewell pat, and picked up the onion and two pimientos he had found. They had been lying inside the crate, like a present. It was past suppertime.

He stopped in the doorway of his building to take a last look at the quiet street. Although this was the island of Manhattan, where millions of people lived, most of the buildings in this small section were wholesale warehouses. The men who sold the fruit and vegetables, cheese and eggs, used only the ground floors of their buildings. They closed off the upper stories, leaving them empty.

One block away, and just as quiet on a Friday night, was the center of the Market—on Washington Street, the street for which the Market was named.

The apartment where Tomás lived was in one of the few apartment buildings left in the Market. Tomás climbed the three flights of stairs, pushed open the door, and stepped into the kitchen. His sister Fernanda looked up. Without asking, he knew what she wanted to know. He shook his head, No, Papa had not come.

Fernanda sat at the kitchen table where she had been leafing through one of her scrapbooks. The scrapbooks were her greatest treasures and she never tired of looking at the colored pictures she had pasted in them. Some were of rooms, with beautiful furniture. Other pages were filled with pictures of flowers, clothes and food. All the pictures had been cut from the magazines that Tomás brought her from time to time.

Whenever Fernanda was unhappy or upset, she opened one of her scrapbooks and imagined herself living in one of the beautiful rooms. She did this quite often.

She was paler than Tomás, and though she was fourteen, her big dark eyes had the wide look of a six year old. The blue nylon dress she wore was too small for her. Papa had bought it as a present long ago, hoping she would wear it when she went walking with him on Sundays. But she had not gone walking with him on Sundays. She would not.

Tomás put the onion and the pimientos on the table.

"Ay, Tomás!" Fernanda whispered.

"What is it? What's wrong?" he asked in Spanish.

"The Super," Fernanda said. "She has been here again."

Tomás dropped into one of the chairs at the table. "What did she say?"

"She said, 'Where is your father? I have not seen him in days.' "

"You didn't tell her!" Tomás held his breath.

"No! I said, 'Papa is working both day and night. That is why you have not seen him.' "

Tomás studied one of the magazine pictures upside down. "You told her right," he said.

"The rent is two weeks due," Fernanda continued. "She says she can wait no longer. She must tell the landlord."

Tomás gave this his full attention. "Papa will come home tonight. Or tomorrow."

"If not," Fernanda said, "I do not know what we will eat. We have only this onion, these pimientos, and a little flour."

"No more rice?"

Fernanda shook her head.

Tomás turned one ear to the door. Someone was mounting the stairs with a slow shuffle. It was the step of Mrs. Malloy, the Superintendent. She swept and mopped the halls and stairs, put out the garbage cans, and once a month collected the rent. Mrs. Malloy had a red, kindly face, a loud kindly voice, and a cat named Clancy.

They heard Mrs. Malloy pause, then sigh with relief as she reached the landing and shuffled along two steps . . . three, four . . . she was going past! No, she was stopping. Breathing heavily, she knocked on their door.

Fernanda looked at Tomás to see whether they were going to answer. Tomás nodded his head, yes. Fernanda opened the door.

Mrs. Malloy shuffled into the kitchen and without greeting either Tomás or Fernanda began talking. "Well, and I took it on myself to call the place where your papa works. I don't like the sound of it, I don't."

She looked in a worried way at the children and eased herself onto the third chair at the kitchen table.

11

"I telephoned the place where your papa works," she said again. "He ain't there any more. They told me he ain't there."

"He has a better job!" Tomás said.

Mrs. Malloy raised her shoulders in such a way that her head half disappeared between her great shoulders, like a turtle's.

"Then I'd like to know what's keeping him from paying the rent?" she asked. "Is he maybe saving up until he has money enough to buy the building?"

"He's too busy!" Tomás shouted. "He's so busy he forgets."

Mrs. Malloy looked at the bare shelves in the kitchen cupboard. She waved a hand at them. "That's for sure! And are you trying to tell me it's the same way he forgets to buy food?"

Tomás had no answer.

Mrs. Malloy shook a forefinger at them. "They haven't seen hide nor hair of him on the job for the last three weeks. Nor have the neighbors. And neither, my lambs, have you." Her voice turned soft. "The Lord love you, both of you, you'll have to face it. Tomás, Fernanda, your papa will not be coming back. Not right away, anyhow. Not soon enough to put any hot food inside the pair of you tonight."

Still Tomás said nothing.

"Mind, I don't say he won't *ever* come back. Only that for the time bein' we've got to find somebody to look after the two of you."

She paused again to catch her breath. The children watched her, wondering what she would say next.

She threw up her hands. "Sure now, you've a nice auntie or an uncle or even a cousin who'd be glad to have you over for a little visit?"

Tomás started to shake his head, but Mrs. Malloy went on.

"Well, then . . . I guess we'll just have to call Welfare on Monday. They take very good care of children at the Shelter, and they'll turn the city upside down to try to find your papa."

Tomás was thinking fast. "Oh, we won't need *Welfare*, Mrs. Malloy. We have a godmother in Brooklyn. She has already asked us to come there," he said without hesitation. "We will go on Sunday."

Mrs. Malloy leaned on the table and pushed herself to her feet. "And why didn't you tell me that right off? And save me all that worryin'?"

Her glance wandered around the kitchen. The gas range and the noisy refrigerator belonged to the landlord. Six plates, three cups, some glasses, bowls, and a few pans sat on the two shelves. The red and chrome table and four chairs were the only furniture in the room. She looked again at the empty cupboard.

"It'll take two shakes of a lamb's tail to heat up some fish cakes. There are plenty left from supper. I'll have Malloy bring them up to you." She turned to leave, then thought of something else. "And don't be worryin' over your furniture. Malloy'll cover it up and store it in the basement where nobody can get at it." She patted Fernanda's shoulder. "It'll be waitin' for you as soon as you come back from Brooklyn."

She opened the door. "And don't you set foot out of this place without givin' me your godmother's name and address. Hear?"

They heard her shuffle down the stairs. When she was out of earshot, Fernanda whispered to Tomás.

"Why did you tell her that, about the godmother?"

He waited to answer until he heard Mrs. Malloy's door slam.

"Because I had to. You don't want to go to Welfare, do you?"

"No," Fernanda answered in Spanish. "I do not want to go anywhere. But I know we cannot stay here. The police will throw us out as they did the Garcías. Tomás," she said, looking hard at her brother, "in the street I shall die." She was about to cry.

"We won't be thrown in the street," Tomás assured her, though he felt far from sure.

He, too, was thinking of the Garcías. Juan García's father had also gone away and not come back. From the window Tomás and Fernanda had watched the Garcías' furniture being put on the street. Then the Welfare came and took the Garcías away. People said Welfare was good, but all Tomás knew for sure was that he never saw Juan García again.

For himself he was not so much afraid as for Fernanda. She was like Clancy, Mrs. Malloy's cat. Clancy was seven. He had been born in Mrs. Malloy's apartment and had never been out of it. Mrs. Malloy said he was an apartment cat.

Fernanda was an apartment girl. She had been born in Puerto Rico. When she was two years old, Papa and

15

Mama and Grandmama had brought her to New York with them. But she didn't remember that. She only knew this apartment on the fifth floor. Papa and Mama worked all day. Grandmama could not climb up and down so many stairs, so she never took Fernanda outdoors.

Soon after Tomás was born, Mama died.

Grandmama took care of Tomás and Fernanda. But she did not send Fernanda to school, because she did not think girls needed to learn to read and write. Fernanda was glad. She was afraid of going out of the house, and the thought of walking through the open streets terrified her. She wanted to stay inside, to be under a roof all the time. She had seen the huge trucks and heard them snorting, honking, hissing, and braking as they roared forward or backed up.

Tomás was different. As soon as he could walk, he had unlatched the door of the apartment, explored the hall, and fallen down a flight of stairs. As soon as he could climb downstairs without falling, he ran away. A neighbor brought him back, but he ran away almost every day after that—and came back every night. When summer came, he played on the streets with the older children from the tenement in the next block, and from them he learned how to dodge cars and trucks.

When he was five, his father said he would have to go to school. He went with two second graders—Juan

García and Raimundo Sánchez who were looked after and bossed by Loretta, Juan's older sister. Mornings, they waited together for the school bus.

Then Grandmama died. That was terrible. Luckily Fernanda had learned how to sew and cook and clean the house. As fast as Tomás learned himself, he taught Fernanda how to speak and to read English. And Papa worked hard to keep his family together. But now Papa was lost.

"Where are we going?" Fernanda asked. "Tomás, what are we going to do?"

"I don't know." He got up from the chair and wandered to the window. The view was a wall, twenty feet away. Its old bricks had turned orange, pink, rich brown and blue. The windows in the wall had iron shutters. One pair unfastened easily. They whined and banged when the wind blew.

Tomás snapped his fingers. "I have an idea. I will tell you in the morning what my idea is."

2

TOMÁS TAKES CHARGE

Tomás woke early and remembered the leftover fish cakes. They had saved two each for breakfast. He jumped out of bed, but instead of running to the kitchen to get them, he ran to look at Papa's bed. The blue bedspread was smooth. The bed was empty.

He went to the kitchen, put water on to boil for the coffee, and then dressed.

While he ate his fish cakes, he thought about his plan. As soon as he finished eating, he told Fernanda he was going out but that he would be back very soon.

Two blocks down Greenwich Street was the apartment house were Raimundo Sánchez had lived. It, too, was sandwiched between warehouses. No children of school age lived in the building now, but Tomás knew that the Pérez and Salvador families lived on the top floor. Their children were babies. Bert, the taxi driver, lived on the third floor.

Tomás ran all the way to this building and climbed up four flights of stairs. There was a shorter flight to

the roof. He made it without meeting anyone.

Unhooking the door, he stepped out onto the flat, tarred roof. The steamy air smelled of tar and the ocean. On one side he looked up at the higher roof of the next building. On the other, a low wall separated the roof he stood on from the roof of the adjoining building. Tomás walked on tiptoe to this wall, stepped on it, and jumped down on the roof below.

Downtown he could see the skyscrapers in the haze. To the west and very close, the Hudson River sparkled where the sun hit it. He looked at the back of a great

neon sign on a roof not far away. At night it changed
from a lemon to an orange, blinking back and forth.

The river was deep here, and wide, already part of
the ocean. On the other side of it, under the giant clock,
was New Jersey. River traffic had stopped for the weekend. The tugboats had docked, their crews gone home.
A white Belgian ship tied to a pier two blocks away
looked near enough for Tomás to be able to jump on
its deck.

Tomás knew all about the building whose roof he
was standing on, because once he and Juan and Rai-

mundo had explored all the buildings in the neighborhood. Only the ground floor of this building was used. Above the ground floor the stairway was boarded over; so was the roof door leading down into the building. All the windows which faced the street were covered with tin. The broken panes of the back windows let in light, air, and pigeons. It would be a perfect place for him and Fernanda to live—and nobody would think of looking for them here.

Tomás headed for the fire escape, the old-fashioned iron-ladder kind, at the back of the building. He climbed down it from the roof and entered the top floor of the building through a broken window. Once inside he made his way to the big front room. A little light crept in through the cracks around the sealed windows. As his eyes grew used to the dim light, he saw a soot-blackened fireplace on the inside wall. Good! They could build a fire, and Fernanda could cook over it, like the Pilgrims.

The floor was thick with soot and grime. A mattress lay opposite the fireplace. It was in pretty good shape, but also covered with soot. Fernanda could clean the floor and the mattress and she could sleep in this room.

Among some junk and broken plaster in one of the other rooms was a pad from a baby's crib. He would have to use that. Also he would clean up that room, and it would be his.

You could lock the door to the front room from the inside. Lucky! If anybody came, he and Fernanda could lock themselves in. He nodded. They would hide here till Papa came home. It might even be fun, like living in a secret tower.

He walked back to the fire-escape window, kicking small chunks of fallen plaster out of his way. The floor was dirty, and glass lay splintered under the three back windows. But light streamed in. From where Tomás stood he could see a wide stretch of sky, a row of tarred roofs, and leaning chimneys.

Most of the windows of the buildings in the back had dirty or missing panes, which meant those floors were empty. One row was tight-shuttered. No one would be able to look in on them.

This will please Fernanda, he thought as he climbed the ladder. She can even have sun and air, without going out to the street, and no people to frighten her.

When he walked into his own kitchen a few minutes later, Fernanda was sitting at the red-topped table, waiting.

He described the place he had found. "We will hide there," he explained. "Papa will surely come in a day or two."

Fernanda wanted to know how Papa would find them.

"How will he find us if Welfare takes us?" Tomás asked. "This way, someone will see me in the street,

23

and they will say, 'Your Papa is looking for you.' Then we will go home."

"I think you are crazy!" Fernanda thrust out her lip and sat looking stubborn.

"Do you want to go to Welfare then?" Tomás asked. "They'll *make* you go to school. To first grade, with little kids. They'll make you *go outside,* too. All the time."

Fernanda's outthrust lower lip went slowly back where it belonged. "Maybe you're not so crazy," she said.

"Just wait!" Tomás said. "You'll like it, you'll see! I bet even Papa will like it so much he'll want to live there with us."

Fernanda closed her scrapbook and leaned back. She gave him a serious look. "Very well, Tomás. We will do as you say."

Tomás slapped the table. "Good! Let's see what we have to take." He jumped up and started for the bedroom.

"Wait!" Fernanda called. "What are we going to eat?"

He came back and perched on the edge of his chair. "Peppers and onions. I found two, I can find more. Other things fall off the trucks and out of baskets. I've seen them. Things Americans eat." He made a face. "Carrots and potatoes and green leaves. If they eat them, we can."

24

Fernanda clapped her hand to her mouth. "Tomás—the godmother in Brooklyn! You told Mrs. Malloy."

"Ah, yes." Tomás scratched his head. Suddenly he nodded. "The telephone book. In a telephone booth in a drug store I have seen a whole book for Brooklyn. I will go and pick out a godmother for Mrs. Malloy."

Fernanda giggled, then shrugged her shoulders.

Tomás jumped up again and went to the cupboard. "We must think what we want to take. Plates." He took two from the shelf. "Two cups, two glasses—" He began bringing the dishes to the table. "It is like moving. We are going to live in a new house."

Fernanda joined the game. She opened two brown paper shopping bags and stood them on the floor. Into one, she put her red dress and her yellow dress, neatly folded, and her most prized article of clothing, her pink quilted nylon robe, a present from Mrs. Malloy. Into the other, she put Tomás's four shirts and three T-shirts, his blue pullover sweater, his other pair of undershorts. She left his winter coat hanging in the closet.

Tomás folded their red blankets, laid two pillows on top and rolled them into a bundle which he tied with rope. He put the bundle on his head. "I'll take these now," he said from under the bundle. "We will have to sleep here tonight—because we told Mrs. Malloy we would leave tomorrow. We'll use the bedding from Papa's bed."

He took the bundles to the vacant building.

In the afternoon he made another trip, carrying a plastic bucket filled with their dishes, glasses, saucepan and frying pan. In the other hand he carried a broom. So far he had met no one to question him or wonder what he was doing. But now, as he was going down the stairs from the roof for the last time, he heard the heavy tread of a man coming up.

Tomás stopped on one foot in the middle of the fourth floor hall. Should he turn around, sneak back up? He leaned over the bannister and peered down. He could see the shine of a metal badge on the man's cap. Then the man moved into the light from the dim bulb in the ceiling of the hall below, and Tomás saw the black crown of a cap and the shoulder of a faded plaid shirt. It was Bert, the taxi driver.

Tomás waited until the door on the third floor closed. The tenants of this building must not see him. Not when he could help it.

When he got back home, he found Mrs. Malloy had sent up some stew. Fernanda turned on the TV while they ate. When they finished and Fernanda had washed the dishes, they lay across Papa's unused bed and watched one program after another until very late. They did not think about Papa's being gone or even about having to hide until he came back.

3

CAVE DWELLERS

The faint, rich tones of the City Hall clock striking ten wakened Tomás on Sunday morning. The sun was streaming between the flowery curtains. He lay looking at the apartment. He imagined how it would look without furniture.

He got up. At the kitchen sink he washed his face and combed his hair. He brushed his teeth, left the toothpaste open for Fernanda, and put his toothbrush in the shopping bag with his clothes.

Fernanda yawned sleepily as she came into the kitchen. She boiled water, and they each drank a cup of black coffee for breakfast. Luckily the big jar of instant coffee was still half full.

"I wish we could take the TV," she said wistfully.

"Well, we can't," Tomás said firmly. "But I'll get you some more old magazines for your scrapbooks."

"My scrapbooks!" Fernanda put her hand over her mouth. "I was forgetting them!"

She ran to her room and returned with her nine

spiral-bound notebooks, her scissors, and a jar of paste. How *could* she have forgotten them! They held her secret life, and all her dreams.

At eleven o'clock when church-going tenants would be at Mass and the others might still be sleeping, Tomás made a trip to the hideout. He took what food remained—half a jar of pickles, a jar of mustard, salt, pepper, a nearly full bottle of oil, a sack of flour. And the precious coffee.

In front of the other building he met Bert.

"Hi, kid, how's tricks?" Bert asked as he walked by.

"Okay." Tomás smiled, and set the shopping bag on the sidewalk as though resting. He waited until Bert had turned the corner before he darted into the hallway.

On the top floor the door to one apartment stood open. Tomás heard voices, but he slipped past without being seen. He crossed the two rooftops, climbed down the fire-escape ladder to the landing and through the window into the back room of the hideout.

In the dark front room, he set the groceries down by the fireplace. He swept a layer of grit from the mattress that Fernanda would sleep on and tried to sweep the room. But he raised such a choking dust that he had to sit in the open back window to wait for it to settle. A pigeon walked babbling along the parapet of the opposite roof. It saw Tomás, paused, and watched him without interest.

Tomás went back into the front room and again

swept up such a dust storm that it almost choked him and he had to leave the hideout. He ran across the roofs and down the stairs. Either the Pérez or the Salvador family—he couldn't tell which—went downstairs ahead of him. He waited a few minutes before going out to the street. Then he raced around the corner.

"Once we're moved in, I won't go out so often," he said to himself. "And when I'm out, I'll stay out. Or maybe I'll only go out late at night after everybody's asleep."

Instead of going straight back to Fernanda, he toured the telephone booths. Sometimes in the coin-return slots he found forgotten dimes.

It was one o'clock when he went into the Chambers Street luncheonette, found a Brooklyn telephone book, and leafed through it. In the R's he found *Mrs. Fernanda Ravello.* Perfect! She could be the godmother Fernanda was named for.

He asked the counterman politely to lend him a pencil. He copied the name and address on a scrap of paper. He deliberately did *not* copy the phone number.

He tucked the paper into his pocket and returned the pencil. He then went on up the street and strolled into every open luncheonette, drug store, and bar. He slid two fingers into the black coin-return cup in every unoccupied telephone booth, was lucky or unlucky, and strolled out again.

Once, a long time ago, he had pressed the coin-return and two quarters, three dimes and a nickel had slipped smoothly into his hand. Today his luck was nothing like that. Only two dimes. But when he added the nickel he had collected for returning a soda bottle left on a loading dock, the total was twenty-five cents.

It was time to go home. As he circled back, he thought how he would spend the money: fifteen cents would buy a pound of beans or a pound of rice, whichever Fernanda wanted. He would let her decide. That left ten cents. With another nickel he could buy half a dozen cracked eggs from the egg wholesaler tomorrow.

Tomás liked arithmetic—even decimals and fractions. He found it useful. He liked knowing that if 15 cents would buy six eggs, 10 cents would buy four. If the wholesale man did not know, Tomás would tell him.

He went up to the apartment and showed Fernanda the day's profit and the name of the godmother.

"She must be a nice lady," Fernanda said.

"Why?"

"She has a nice name."

Tomás smiled and looked up from stacking the two dimes and the nickel.

"Anything to eat?"

"Peppers and onion," Fernanda said. While Tomás was out she had sliced them into a pan with water and put it on the stove to stew. She had found one dried-up frankfurter at the back of the refrigerator, sliced that,

tic. Red roses on the table made every meal like a party. Between the plastic curtains, red plastic geraniums on the window sills never withered, never stopped blooming. Plastic lace doilies on the television and on the end tables made white curlicues against the dark wood. Green plastic ivy curled around the blue television lamp.

Tomás touched the harmless thorns of the roses in their plastic basket.

Clancy rubbed against Tomás's leg and purred, wanting to lick the bowl.

"Clancy," Tomás said, "you're too fat."

Tomás scraped the bowl, licked the spoon, and sat back, swinging his legs. Ice cream certainly tasted better than carrots.

He wished he wasn't so worried.

"Come," he said to Fernanda, "we better go."

Mrs. Malloy put the paper with the godmother's name and address into a drawer.

"Now, don't worry. Either of you," she said. "I'll phone you or your papa will, soon as he comes home. You'll just be gone long enough for a nice little visit."

Tomás nodded. Mrs. Malloy patted his head and kissed Fernanda's cheek. Fernanda's sad, frightened eyes filled with tears.

"Don't worry. There's nothing to worry about. Honest," Mrs. Malloy told her. "You kids are gonna have a wonderful time in Brooklyn."

"And don't get on the wrong subway," said Mr. Malloy, turning his head from the television for the first time.

Mrs. Malloy watched them down the steps. Tomás called goodbye. When they were out of sight, they heard the door close. Fernanda hesitated.

"Come on," he said, and took her hand.

Fernanda behaved all right until Tomás opened the street door. Then she put her back against the wall.

"No!" she cried.

Tomás shushed her. He was afraid she would bolt back upstairs the way Clancy did.

"Come on," he whispered fiercely. "You cannot go back now. Mrs. Malloy will find out we told a lie. She will call Welfare."

"I am afraid," Fernanda whimpered.

"You must come. You have to," Tomás said, "even if you are afraid. Terrible things will happen to us if you do not."

He dug in his shopping bag and pulled out his sweater. He put it over her head, like a kerchief, tying the sleeves loosely under her chin. "Come on. That's a magic sweater. With than on, nobody can see you. Shut your eyes."

He opened the door and pushed her ahead of him onto the sidewalk. The door banged shut.

Hand in hand, each carrying a shopping bag, they started down the street.

"Just a little further," he said soothingly. "Just one more block."

She held his fingers in so tight a grip that they hurt, but he dared not say so.

At last they reached the other building. They had gone up one flight when they heard people coming in below. Fernanda went up the steps like a frightened cat.

At the door to the roof Tomás whispered, "Open it."

She stepped out on the roof. "No!" she gasped, and turned back. Tomás blocked the way.

"Go on!" he said in a whisper. He shoved her out and closed the door behind him.

Fernanda shrank against the door frame. Tomás understood a little of how she must feel. Up here, out of the shadowy canyons of warehouses and buildings, the sky was still light. It spread overhead, roofless, surrounding them in every direction.

"Come on," he urged.

Fernanda whimpered, pressing tighter against the wall. Tomás opened the door a crack. In the hall below was the Salvador family. Mr. Salvador was turning the key in their lock.

Tomás shut the door again and waved Fernanda toward the other roof.

"Come on. Before those people hear us."

He took her hand and pulled. Once away from the wall, she moved willingly enough, though he could feel her terror in her stiff fingers.

"Just a little further," he coaxed. "We're almost there."

When they reached the fire-escape ladder, he took her shopping bag.

"Climb down to the iron landing," he whispered to her. "Wait for me there."

Tomás put the two shopping bags near the edge of the roof where he could reach them, climbed partway down the ladder and picked up the bags again.

"Here," he said, handing them down to Fernanda. "Take them. Let go the railing! You can't fall."

She did as he told her, but she gasped and clutched the railing as he landed beside her with a jump that shook the iron slats of the landing.

"All right, all right," he said. "Go on in. I'm right behind you. As soon as we get inside I'll light a candle."

She crouched on the window sill, reached one foot tentatively down to the floor, said, "Ah," as she felt it, and stepped inside.

Tomás crawled in after her. He stood shifting his feet uncomfortably on the rubble-covered floor while he hunted for matches and a candle.

"Is this it?" she whispered.

"Yes. It's dark in here now, but in the morning you'll see how nice it is. Now we go up front."

In the front room she stood peering around.

"Put your bag down," he said. He ran over and shot the bolt on the door. "See, even a lock." He spread his arms. "Nice, eh? You like it, don't you? *Don't* you, Fernanda?"

Fernanda put her shopping bag on the floor, leaning it against her leg. "I don't know." But she was beginning to feel safe again. The brown walls and dirty floor made the room seem like a cave.

Tomás knelt by the fireplace and struck a match. The paper he had thrown into it while cleaning, caught fire and gave off an orange glow.

Fernanda's great dark eyes reflected the fire. Light fell on her smooth pale cheeks and forehead, on the black hair framing her face. Tomás remembered a picture of people dressed in skins standing around a fire.

"You look just like a cave dweller," he cried. He sat back on the floor, hugging his knees. "We're both cave dwellers."

Fernanda crouched in front of the fire beside him.

"Well?" he demanded. "Do you like it?"

"Yes." Now she was smiling faintly. She rubbed one finger along a floor board. "It is *very* dirty." Tomás knew she was thinking pleasurably of sweeping it.

She looked around. "Is there something to sit on?"

"Sit on this." He dragged forward the mattress on which he had spread some bedding. "Tomorrow I'll get some boxes to sit on and to put things in."

He fished in his shopping bag and took out the second sack of potato chips. *"Mira."* He handed them to Fernanda. "Look, a surprise!"

Fernanda laughed and smoothed back her hair. Her teeth glinted as she bit the cellophane and tore open the bag. "What a day! Potato chips and ice cream both. But I am sorry we lied to Mrs. Malloy."

Tomás nodded. "Me, too. But when Papa comes back next week, she'll be glad she didn't give us to Welfare."

"Is this room always so dark?"

"Just about," Tomás said. "This will be your sleeping cave. I will sleep in the next room. It gets light out that way." He nodded toward the back.

"Where will I cook?" she asked.

"In the fireplace."

Fernanda looked at him. "How?"

"*How?*" Tomás shouted. "The way the Cave women did, and pioneers and Puritans. Everybody used to. If you'd go to school, you wouldn't be so dumb."

Fernanda got up without saying anything and went to her bed. The fire had died down, and the room grew black again.

Tomás stood up. "Do you want the candle?" Fernanda did not answer so he took it with him into the room that was to be his.

He blew out the candle and lay down on his hard mattress feeling pleased. The things they needed were here; Fernanda was here. They were safe. All they had to do now was keep hidden till Papa came back.

The noises of the Market sounded far away. Then something scuttled inside the wall. He listened. A small animal ran across the roof. The scrabbling in the wall changed to gnawing.

"What's that?" Fernanda called out in alarm.

"Must be rats," he called back. "Don't be afraid. Tomorrow I'll get a cat."

Reassured, Fernanda lay down again, and in a little while they were both asleep.

4

FOOD, FIRE, WATER

The next morning in the gray light that leaked in from around the windows, it took Tomás a few seconds to remember where he was. He turned over.

Fernanda was already awake and called out to him, "Where's the bathroom?"

"Out there. The bathroom is in the hall."

She got up, put on her dress, and unlocked the door. He heard plaster crunching under her feet as she walked down the hall. But in a minute she was back.

"Tomás—" She stopped in the doorway. "Tomás, there's no water! None in the sink or in the bathroom."

Tomás jumped up. "Water! I never thought of it."

He started for the kitchen. Fernanda followed.

"We can not wash or make coffee! What are we going to do?" she demanded. "How can we live here?"

Tomás turned on the faucets in the sink. No water. Under the sink he ran his hand down the pipe until it touched a small, round wheel which he began to turn. It turned easily. Fernanda stopped talking. She watched the sink, but no water spurted from the faucets.

"Ay," she sighed. "I wish it was true that we did have a godmother in Brooklyn."

"You don't even know where Brooklyn is," Tomás reminded her crossly.

She clasped her hands and looked out at the early-morning sky. "But it is nice here," she said.

Tomás stood thinking. One time last winter in the other building there had been trouble with the water. He had followed the plumber from floor to floor. He remembered there had been a valve on a lower floor which turned all the water off and on at once. If this building had such a valve, perhaps he could turn the water on now.

He made his way down the dark, dirty stairs, flight by flight. He searched for the valve on each floor. I should have thought of water, he scolded himself. This camping is not easy.

He found the valve he was looking for on the lowest of the closed-off floors, in the kitchen beside the sink. But when he tried to turn it, it refused to budge.

Very well, he could take care of that. Again he went from floor to floor until he found a scrap of wire and two small boards. The boards were about a foot long and an inch thick. He fastened them loosely together with the wire. Raimundo had taught him last summer how to use such a homemade wrench to unscrew the big bolt on the fire hydrant so they could play in the water.

44

He took his wrench back downstairs again and forced the valve to turn. A sound of rattling in the pipes rewarded him. Water was beginning to flow.

"Whew!" he said, sitting back and listening to the chug, pop, and bang as the water forced air out of the pipes.

Upstairs he found Fernanda watching brown water spurt from the choking sink faucets. In the bathroom he heard the tank filling.

He brought more scraps of wood up from the floor below where he also found some bricks and an old icebox grill. He carried these up and put two bricks in the fireplace. He set the grill on top of them and built a fire in between.

In the kitchen, the water was running clear. Fernanda was washing her hands and face at the sink. He saw she had braided her hair—a good sign.

"We forgot the soap," she exclaimed.

"I will buy some," Tomás said grandly. He filled a pan with water for coffee. "Your stove is ready. Come see."

When the water boiled, they made their coffee and went to sit in the back windows to drink it. Today the air, blowing fresh from the sea, made breathing a pleasure.

Tomás produced the nickel from his pocket and showed it to Fernanda. "Do you want soap—or rice? I have to find at least another nickel before I can get either one."

"Soap," she said.

"Oh, Fernanda, you always want everything so clean. I'm hungry."

"Then get rice," Fernanda said.

Crossing the roofs, Tomás realized it was very early, too early to buy rice. The big passenger liners were just coming up the river. When the first one was near enough for him to read the name on the bow he saw it was the *Constitution*. The *Leonardo* was close behind. He watched until a high building hid them from view. Then he went downstairs.

He would look around for boxes to use as furniture. A crisp pimiento lay in the middle of the street. Wondering how it had escaped the wheels of the trucks, he picked it up. Farther on, he found another. Then in the gutter, two sweet potatoes. He picked up an empty onion bag of purple mesh and put the vegetables in it.

At the corner he stared in delight. Here were riches: the street cleaners had made a big pile of broken crates, cartons, paper, cardboard, and discarded fruits and vegetables. He picked out a long green fruit which felt furry and a small yellow one which felt smooth and dusty.

"Finding anything, kid?"

Tomás jumped. It was the street cleaner. He showed him the yellow and green fruit. "What are these?" he asked.

"Squash," the street cleaner answered. "That's zucchini—" he pointed to the green one. "I don't know what the other one's called. It's good for you, though." He took off his glove and patted Tomás's thick hair. "Make your hair curl." He winked.

Tomás smiled back. "Does it have vitamins?"

"It's jumping with vitamins."

The street cleaner turned his back and began to

push his broom along the gutter. Then he stopped and looked back.

"There are some bananas down at the corner, if you want them." He pointed to the corner.

Tomás saw a pile of green and black banana stalks against a building.

"Thanks!" he shouted, running toward them, swinging the purple bag.

Sure enough, next to the stalks Tomás found two barrels full of green and yellow bananas and shredded paper. Every banana was damaged, its yellow skin bruised black or torn open, but parts looked good. Tomás peeled one, broke off the good part, and tasted it. His brown eyes widened. It *was* good! He could hardly believe they were being thrown out.

His mouth full of banana, his eyes sparkling, he looked like a chipmunk.

He dug down into each barrel as far as he could reach and filled the bag in no time at all. When he picked it up, it was heavy.

He had wanted to take up some wood for the fireplace, and two boxes to sit on. He also had to buy rice. There was no other way: he would have to make two trips.

On the way back, he found a clean crate and four Coke bottles. After putting the bag of bananas and vegetables into the crate, he promptly turned the Coke bottles into cash. Then, carrying the crate in both arms, he started upstairs.

His timing was wrong. As he set foot on the third floor, Bert's door opened. Bert came out, settling his taxi-driver hat on his head.

"Hiya, kid," Bert shouted.

Tomás backed against the wall for Bert to pass.

"You're getting to be quite a visitor," Bert said jovially.

Tomás gulped. At that instant a door slammed on the top floor. He heard the quick tap of high-heeled shoes on the stairs and saw the round brown calves and tiny feet of Mrs. Pérez.

"I'm baby-sitting for Mrs. Pérez," Tomás said. He spoke rapidly so Mrs. Pérez, who might speak English, would not understand.

"Good for you," Bert said. He poked the sack. "What you got there?"

"Bananas. For the baby. Want one?"

"Naw. Just had my coffee."

Mrs. Pérez reached the third floor landing. Bert turned and lifted his cap. "Morning, ma'am."

"Good morning," she answered.

Tomás spoke rapidly to her in Spanish. Bert caught the word '*bebé* sitter' as he plunged on downstairs.

Tomás was asking Mrs. Pérez if she needed a baby sitter.

She looked at him, surprised. "Not today," she said.

"Perhaps tomorrow?" Tomás suggested.

"*Sí,* tomorrow. Perhaps." She, too, hurried downstairs.

Tomás chuckled as he lugged the box and bananas on up to the roof. Now he had an excuse for being there. Perhaps Mrs. Pérez or Mrs. Salvador would let him baby sit. He would ask them every morning.

He was tiptoeing across the roof when white smoke began to pour out of the chimney above their hideout. He gasped. The watchman, the tenants from this building, anyone who happened to be looking, could see it.

As fast as he could he hurried down to Fernanda.

"What did you put on the fire?" he shouted.

"Some dirty old papers. Why?"

"It's smoking like crazy." He ran to the front room. He struck a match to the smoldering papers and flames leapt up, driving one large puff of smoke out into the room. "Like a smoke signal," he thought, "like a smoke signal to Welfare."

He went to the back room and knelt beside the window for a while, watching to see if anyone was going to come. Nothing happened. He sighed with relief and took the bananas out of the crate.

Fernanda was astonished to see so many.

They peeled one after another and ate and laughed until they were full. And still there were five bananas left. Tomás started to put them on the shelf above the sink.

"Wait," Fernanda cried. She wrung out a gray rag and wiped it across the shelf. The rag came away covered with black mud.

"Ugh!" she said, wrinkling her nose. "Everything here is so dirty."

"What if we wash the floor?" Tomás asked. "Then there will be no dust."

"We'll have mud!" Fernanda said. The job looked so hopeless she shrugged her shoulders and began to laugh. "If Mrs. Malloy could see us now." She giggled, throwing up her hands the way Mrs. Malloy did.

"We have water and a cooking place, and bananas," Tomás said gaily. "Now I'm going out to buy rice."

5

A COOKSTOVE

Monday passed, and Tuesday and Wednesday. Each morning Tomás found more fruit and vegetables than he and Fernanda could eat. Sometimes he found whole boxfuls stacked on the curb, waiting for the garbage trucks.

One morning he found a box of pears. Half were brown and mushy, but some were yellow—ripe and juicy, perfect for eating.

The first time he brought Fernanda two cucumbers he asked anxiously, "Can you cut off that soft part? Is the other part still good?"

"It looks good," she said. "Wait a moment."

She ran from the open-air back room through the hall to the cave room. Tomás stared after her frowning, trying to remember. No, he thought, slowly nodding his head, I have never seen her run before. She has always crept about with a shuffle like Grandmama.

She came flying back with one of the brown-covered spiral books and began leafing through the colored

53

pages of pictures. She found the one she was hunting for and pointed at it. A great copper-colored pot filled the page. In it orange and green vegetables floated in a brown sauce.

"There," she said. "What does that say?"

Tomás smacked his lips. "Can you make that?"

"Maybe, if the butcher would give you a bone for broth. What does it say?"

"You read it," Tomás insisted.

As soon as he had begun to read in first grade, he had brought his books home to show Fernanda. In his pride at learning CAT and HEN and THE, he had taught her the words and awakened her interest in reading and spelling. She understood what she read, but she had trouble saying the English words aloud.

"Stew of spring vegetables," she read slowly, pronouncing with difficulty the list of things needed to make it. "Can you find some of these?" she asked.

Most of them he had never heard of, but he promised to try. "Anyway, it says here," he pointed out, "almost all vegetables go well in a stew."

The butcher gave him a nice meaty bone. He searched till he found carrots, an onion, a potato, some stalks of celery, and green peppers. The stew did not look as pretty as the one in the picture, but it tasted good. Fernanda was terribly proud.

"It's good like Mrs. Malloy's," she said.

"Better!" Tomás declared.

He had never been so busy. He quickly learned the habits of everyone in the building. Whenever he chanced to meet Mrs. Pérez or Mrs. Salvador, he asked if they wanted a baby sitter. On Wednesday, Mrs. Pérez said yes. He stayed with three-year-old Fidel while she went shopping.

She paid him enough to buy soap and bread and candy.

On Thursday he spent the afternoon watching both little Fidel and the Salvador baby while their mothers went to a movie. Both women thought he still lived in Mrs. Malloy's building.

With that day's money in his pocket, he walked to Canal Street. He bought candles. At the secondhand bookstore he bought Fernanda an old magazine. He had money left over! He jingled it in his pocket and walked home whistling.

He felt very pleased with himself. He could do as well as Papa at providing for them. Except a television set. We have not been hungry all week though, he thought. Before, we were often hungry.

They had been careful not to light fires until after dark when the smoke could not be seen. They missed their hot morning coffee, but Tomás solved that problem, too.

Several blocks down the street stood the warehouse of a company which collected waste paper. When their trucks brought other trash, it was piled overnight on the sidewalk. Tomás began to visit the place every evening.

He found a little office chair with four wheels, the leather seat only a little torn. He took it home. The following evening under piles of wooden packing boxes and neon tubes, he found a cup and two pie tins. On Friday night he made his best find—a small kerosene stove with two burners, and yards and yards of yellow cloth.

He was so excited he couldn't think. How could he carry the stove and the cloth? How could he carry even the stove to the hideout? Yet how could he leave the yellow cloth behind? He danced about looking for something to haul the stove on, wishing he had a wire shopping cart with wheels.

He spotted an end of clothesline rope and pulled at it. It turned out to be long enough to tie around the stove. Could he then hoist it on his shoulders, the way he'd seen movers do?

He was wrapping it around the stove when a worker from the Market came along. He didn't seem to be in a hurry. Tomás felt in his pocket. A dime and a quarter. He looked back and forth from the stove to the cloth and made up his mind.

He stepped in front of the man.

"Hey, mister," he said, "could you help me carry that? Just down the street? The Con-Ed's shut off our gas. My mother's got nothing to cook on."

"Carry what?"

"This." Tomás put a finger on the stove. "Look, I'll give you this yellow cloth."

The man looked at the cloth.

"I was gonna give it to my mother, but she'd rather have the stove," Tomás said.

The man smiled. "You keep that pretty silk, son."

He unwound the clothesline from around the stove and handed it to Tomás. He lifted the two-burner kerosene stove to his shoulders as though it were an empty bushel basket.

"Where do you live?" he asked.

"Just down a couple of blocks." Tomás wadded the cloth into a bundle, tied it with the clothesline, and led the way.

In the time it took to walk the five blocks home, Tomás figured out what to tell the man.

"We live on the top floor," he said apologetically.

"I guess you know kerosene stoves is against the law," the man said.

Tomás nodded. "The landlord's coming for the rent. I guess he shouldn't see the stove."

The man shook his head. "Unh-unh!"

"Could you put it on the roof? He won't go up there."

The man chuckled. "You are a right smart boy, son! When you grow up, your mama won't have to worry about no Con Eds and no landlord, neither."

He carried the little stove all the way to the top of

the building and out onto the roof. "You be careful, first time you light that," he warned. "It's liable to smoke like the old devil." He refused to take the yellow cloth. He refused the dime, too.

"Thanks, mister," Tomás said, "Thanks a lot."

"Glad to help," he said.

First, Tomás took the cloth down to Fernanda, and then the can that held kerosene and fitted on the end of the stove. Last of all, he tied the clothesline around the stove itself and lowered it over the edge of the roof like a crane unloading cargo. Fernanda helped him lift it through the window.

6

BEWARE! THE WATCHMAN

The next morning Tomás was crossing the roof with a gallon jug of kerosene he'd just bought at a service station on Chambers Street. He and Fernanda had been hiding for nearly a week now, and he had been going back and forth across the roof so often that he felt safe. He had grown careless, not bothering to check the blind windows across the back court or the other rooftops before showing himself.

Instead, thinking of lighting the new stove, he began to whistle. Fernanda could heat water to wash their clothes. He might even take a bath. He could pour a bucketful of hot water into the square iron washtub which stood on legs next to the sink and bathe in it.

"Hey, you—git off there!"

Tomás jumped. His whistle died in a gasp. He felt as conspicuous as a cat crossing an empty street. As he turned to hurry back toward the apartment house, he stumbled and the bottle of kerosene slipped from his hand. It fell on the tarpaper roof with a clunk. He bent to pick it up. The hot roof . . . the sun . . . the kerosene! What if the bottle was broken?

When he straightened up, the bottle again safe in his hands and unbroken, he dared to see who was shouting. He saw a man in a white shirt on one of the roofs across the court. The Market watchman!

Tomás knew him by sight—a small, mean-faced young man. His blue car could be seen cruising the streets on Friday and Saturday nights. He guarded the brown paper bags of potatoes stacked on the sidewalks, the red and white and purple bags of onions. He knew who belonged on the streets and who did not.

Tomás scurried back to the adjoining roof. He ran away from the hideout the way a meadowlark leads people away from her nest. No time to warn Fernanda. He hoped she had heard the watchman's shout and would have sense enough to take everything to the cave room and lock the door.

Quietly he opened the metal-covered roof door and stepped inside. He stood panting, trying to quiet his pounding heart. He still held the jug, which was dangerous. To get caught with kerosene would demand all sorts of explanations. He must get rid of it. But where? If he put it outside someone's door, it might get taken and he would lose fifty cents' worth of good kerosene.

He opened the door cautiously and peeked out. The watchman no longer stood on the other roof. Tomás knew the man could not cross over to the roofs on his side of the block. He would have to go downstairs and drive or walk around to this building.

Tomás stepped out onto the roof and looked for something to climb on. He found a backless chair, weathered gray. He set it next to the chimney. Carrying the bottle in both hands, he stepped up on the chair and set the bottle down behind the chimney. Then he went back inside and walked downstairs. Tomás peered out the open front door. The watchman had seen him. What now? He wanted to run away to where the watchman did not watch. But that was impossible. He had to guard the hideout and Fernanda.

A block away, the car slid into the empty street and rolled toward him. Tomás pretended to be looking for something in a garbage can.

The blue car pulled to the curb. The door slammed. Tomás was afraid to look, but he knew he must. He had to act as though he had nothing to hide, as though he had a clear conscience.

The watchman came toward him with long strides. When he spoke, his voice was angry. "What were you doing up on the roof?"

Tomás made his eyes big and innocent. *"No comprendo."*

The man's face turned pink. "Don't give me that!" he shouted. "You speak English. What were you doing up there?"

Tomás hung his head. "Nothing."

"Nothing! You know you can get shot walking around on roofs? That's private property. What were you looking for? Something to steal?"

"No!" Tomás became indignant.

"What were you doing, then?"

"Nothing!"

"You were carrying something."

Tomás struggled to think of something safe he might have been carrying.

"I had a book! And—and a jug of water."

The man snorted.

"It's true," Tomás cried. "I was looking for a place to sit and read. Without somebody always bothering me."

"Find some other place," the watchman ordered. "You won't find it so quiet getting shot at." He turned away and headed back to his car.

Harry, the garlic man, rose suddenly from a steel door in the sidewalk. The door led down steep steps to a basement. There, the garlic that arrived in big wicker baskets was poured onto a moving belt, and as the garlic bulbs rode along, workers picked them off and popped them, two by two, into neat little boxes which said *HARRY'S SELECTED GARLIC* on each end. Harry was skinny and flat-chested in his white apron. He waved at the watchman, and the watchman waved back.

Tomás's face grew hot. He hated the watchman. Look at him, waving like he was nice and friendly, when he wasn't. He was mean. He couldn't shoot. He wasn't even wearing a gun.

The car drove away, and Tomás kicked the garbage can. Then he dived into the hall and flew upstairs. From now on he would have to be more careful. He hoped Papa would not stay away much longer.

He picked up the kerosene jug and ran with it across the roofs and down the fire escape. He made sure he reached the hideout before the watchman could get back to the roof and catch him.

Sure enough, Fernanda had heard the shout and had locked herself in the cave room. When Tomás called, she opened the door a crack and looked at him fearfully.

"What happened? Who shouted?"

"Let me in," he whispered, panting.

He slipped gratefully into the safe, half-dark cave room, and she bolted the door behind him. He wiped his forehead with his sleeve and sank onto her bed, now covered, like his, with the silky yellow cloth.

"The watchman saw me," he began. "I'm glad you hid. That's what you're supposed to do."

He told her how the watchman had shouted and what he had said.

"I'm staying in the rest of today."

After a while when Tomás was sure it was safe, they

ventured back to the kitchen, keeping well away from the open windows.

Thoughtfully, Tomás said, "I wish I knew why he was up there. Then I'd know if he'll be going back."

He peeled a banana and began to eat it. "Until now we were only hiding from the Malloys and Welfare, but now I got somebody else to hide from—the watchman."

"But we have a stove," Fernanda reminded him. "That will make things better. Let's try it."

"No!" Tomás shook his head violently. "It might smoke at first. Do you want the fire engines to come?"

"Oh, you're so bossy!" she complained, walking away.

A soft rain began drifting out of the sky. Tomás watched it sifting against the black shutters opposite them.

"It's a good day to stay in," he said in his friendliest voice.

Fernanda went to the cave and came back with the new magazine and her scrapbooks. She spread a layer of newspapers on the floor. Tomás mixed a fresh batch of flour-and-water paste, and they played the magazine game.

They looked at each page, studied all the pictures, and read the ads. Fernanda coaxed him to read the stories aloud.

When they grew hungry at midday, they ate more bananas. Fernanda made a salad with two kinds of lettuce, tomato, cucumber, oil, and lemon juice. Except for the bowl, it looked like one shown in the magazine. Tomás had found everything except the oil.

He had worked hard Friday morning to find enough food to last the weekend, for he knew that by Friday night the big, round brooms of the sanitation machines would have scoured the streets bare of food.

Tomás and Fernanda carefully carried the stove into the light, and admired it—front, side, top, back. A metal plate screwed to the back told how to light it.

The rain had stopped as quietly as it began, but darkness came early. As the light faded, Tomás felt safer: at night the watchman guarded the onions and potatoes down on the street.

Tomás sat in one of the windows, watching the night arrive. And listening to it. From somewhere came a slow drip. Across the court he heard pigeons gargling in a nest behind an iron shutter.

Fernanda stood beside him.

"Soon now?" she asked.

"As soon as it's too dark to see smoke."

"*Mira*. Look!" She pointed. Two floors below, a rat ran along a big pipe and scuttled through a tin gutter at the edge of a roof. It drank from a puddle of water and returned the way it came.

Fernanda said, "You forgot to get a cat."

"It's not so easy," Tomás said in his own defense. "You think I can just stand in the street and call kitty, kitty, kitty, and cats will come running? Hah, if it's so easy, *you* do it."

"Maybe I will," she replied.

"Hah!" Tomás said again.

They watched darkness cover the buildings. "If we were sitting on the roof, we could see the river," Tomás said.

"But what if someone saw us?"

"They can't now. It's too dark."

Fernanda was silent a moment. "I'll go," she said.

"What?" Tomás could not believe his ears.

"I mean I might go," she said. "If you'll stay beside me."

"Sure!" He jumped up. "Come on."

They sat with their backs against a chimney.

"Boy, it would take a whole army of helicopters to see us," Tomás bragged.

"So that's the river," Fernanda said. "I was too frightened to look when I first came. It looks nearby and far away at the same time."

"I know. It's because this side *is* close, and that side is 'way over in New Jersey," Tomás explained.

They could see the Statue of Liberty holding her light, but the river lay as gray and empty as the Market's cobblestone streets.

"The ships have all gone home now," Tomás said. "You should see it in the daytime. Ferries and tugboats and barges and *big* ships, bigger than this whole block. And overhead an old helicopter goes whirring and whirring. It has a propeller at the back and one at the front."

At last Tomás decided it was dark enough to light the stove. They went back inside and by candlelight he reread the instructions. Tomás turned the handle that let the kerosene run from the tank to the burner. Then he waited, as the instructions directed. When he thought it was long enough, he turned the lever that raised the tin chimney and allowed him to light the wick.

"Stand back," he ordered Fernanda as he held the match to it. The flame caught and crept around the whole circle of the wick. He lowered the chimney back into place, and through the little isinglass window he watched the flame turn from yellow to blue. He put his hand over the burner but drew it back quickly.

"It's hot!" he said.

On one burner they put a pan of water, on the other a bucket of water, and took turns sticking a finger into the water to see how hot it was getting. Soon the water in the pan began to boil.

"Let's cook something," Tomás said.

"We haven't had supper yet," Fernanda remembered.

"Fried eggs," Tomás said dreamily. "Fried eggs and potatoes. Could you fry potatoes, the way they do in the luncheonette?"

"I could fry bananas," Fernanda suggested.

"Yes!"

When Fernanda put the food on the table, Tomás sat down on his crate, leaned back against the wall, and looked around with a happy sigh. He sniffed the food expectantly.

Fernanda sat down and Tomás took a big bite of banana. "Won't Papa be surprised?" he said with his mouth full.

Fernanda looked up from her plate. "What if he isn't coming back?"

"He *is* coming back!" Tomás shouted, and then clapped his hand over his mouth, remembering it was not safe to make so much noise. "Well, he is," he said more quietly.

Fernanda said nothing.

After supper, she washed the dishes in hot water. She had become used to working by candlelight. They heated more water, and Tomás took a bath. Then he went to bed.

The rain began again. Tomás lay listening to the drops pattering on the tin window-coverings. He felt warm and clean and not the least bit hungry. What if Fernanda was right, and Papa did not come back?

They would live here forever, just like this.

7

SABERTOOTH

On Sunday morning when Tomás made his usual trip to the street, the air smelled cool and clean, and it was so clear that the city looked freshly washed. White gulls sunned themselves on the roofs of the dock buildings, and high up to the north a sprinkling of tame pigeons wheeled and flashed.

Tomás felt good. He took a deep breath before he started down the street toward the dump. It was always possible that he had overlooked something on Friday night.

He rummaged around among strips of carpet and found two magazines and a pretty tin box decorated with pictures of cookies. The cookies made him realize he was hungry.

Fernanda had said she was going to wash her hair. She will be sitting in the window, drying it, he thought. Somehow I'll sneak the pretty tin box in and, when she's not looking, put it on the table.

But when he got to their hideout, Fernanda was not

sitting in any of the windows. He put the box on the fire-escape landing, out of sight against the wall. Fernanda would not be able to see it unless she stuck her head out.

She must be in the kitchen, Tomás thought, and she was certainly being very quiet. But the kitchen was empty.

Strange, he thought. She must be in the cave.

"Fernanda," he called softly, and went to look.

The cave room had no furniture except the bed and a few clothes hanging on nails. No Fernanda. Her bed under its yellow spread was smooth.

"Fernanda," he called again, beginning to worry.

He tiptoed part way down the dark staircase, holding the bannister to keep from slipping on chunks of plaster. He could see the hall below. At least she had not fallen downstairs.

He returned to the kitchen and was standing in the middle of the room biting his lip, wondering what to do, when he heard a noise. He listened. *Someone* was down there. He stood where he was, absorbed in listening.

It *must* be Fernanda. He opened the hall door again, and went out to lean over the bannister.

"Fernanda?" he said in a loud whisper.

"Oh, Tomás!" He saw her now, coming up the stairs. She looked excited and happy.

"Tomás," she called again. *"Mira!"* She was cuddling

74

something in both hands. "Look!" she cried, holding
her hands out to him.

It was a kitten.

He forgot how she had frightened him. He forgot to
be angry.

"Where did you get it?" he asked, reaching for it.

Its round blue eyes stared at him.

"Here, you may hold it," Fernanda said, and put the kitten into his arms. Its orange fur felt soft. Inside its round body, the bones felt soft, too. It scratched at his shirt front, mewing angrily.

"Ah, look at its little claws." He chuckled. "Where did you get it?"

"Downstairs. Oh, isn't it a darling, Tomás!

"I was looking out the window," she said. "I saw a cat run along the ledge. Down there. It jumped through a window into our building. I took a little stew in my bowl and called her. I found her on the second floor. With this kitten! The kitten hid, but I got it. I gave the mother the stew. I will get the bowl later."

At that moment, with a *meow,* the mother cat walked into the room. She rubbed against Fernanda's leg, purring. She was gray and white, and the tip of her tail was crooked.

"Do you want your baby?" Fernanda asked. Taking the kitten from Tomás, she held it before the cat's nose. "If you want it, you'll have to live with us, too."

The cat rubbed its ear against Fernanda's hand. Satisfied that her kitten was safe, she crossed the room to the window, jumped onto the sunny sill, and began washing herself.

Fernanda set the kitten on the floor. It took three unsteady steps and began chasing its orange tail. Tomás could not keep from scooping it up.

"We'll keep them both!" he cried. "The mother can catch rats."

"We can name them," Fernanda said delightedly.

"Sure," Tomás said. "You can name the mother because she's a girl, and I will name the kitten. Okay?"

"Okay."

Tomás held the kitten at arm's length and growled at it. "We're cave dwellers, see? And this is our pet tiger cub. So I'm going to call it Sabertooth!"

Fernanda thought. "I would like to name the mother McCall."

"McCall?" Tomás hooted. "What kind of a name is that?"

"The name of a magazine," Fernanda reminded him. "A woman's magazine. For a woman cat."

Tomás began to giggle.

She pretended not to notice. She held her hand out to the cat. "McCall! Here, McCall!"

Tomás laughed so hard he had to cross his arms over his stomach.

The cat jumped from the window sill and again rubbed herself against Fernanda's leg.

Tomás stopped laughing.

He remembered the cookie tin and the two magazines and ran to fetch them.

Fernanda's cheeks went pink with pleasure. "Oh," she laughed, "here are so many things to enjoy I don't know where to start."

The cats were a wonderful addition to their lives. They made Tomás and Fernanda feel like a family. They kept Fernanda company when Tomás was away, and, having Sabertooth to play with, Tomás did not feel so restless when he had to stay indoors.

Tomás thought McCall must belong to one of the warehouses, but she seemed to go there only for extra meals. The rest of the time she remained in the hideout. She dozed on the window sill in the day and caught rats at night. Three mornings in a row she brought dead rats to Fernanda, and mistook Fernanda's gasps at the sight of them for sounds of delight. Tomás hoped she would run out of rats. He was the one who had to take them to the trash can.

8

FISH

On Wednesday of that week Tomás was out walking along his usual route after the Market had closed, swinging his mesh sack half filled with pimientos and dark green bell peppers. In the bottom was the can of milk he had bought earlier for Sabertooth.

As he rounded a corner, he came upon a woman sorting through a bushel of green beans. He had begun to know that other people besides himself fed their families from what the Market threw away.

"Want some beans, son?" the woman asked. "Help yourself."

She was grandmother-shaped, short and plump. Tomás's eyes came level with her shoulder. Against her light blue summer dress her arms and face gleamed as soft and brown as chocolate.

Tomás began picking out good beans and putting them in his sack.

"I'd like to get about a pound of these," his new friend said. "Then I'm going over to the Fish Market and get me some fish."

Tomás stopped picking out good beans. "You mean there's a place where they throw away fish?"

"Sure there is, honey." She tossed a last bean into her shopping bag. "I'm going there now. You come along if you want to. We'll both get us some fish, if it ain't too late."

"Okay!" Tomás did a jump and skip. How surprised Fernanda would be! And McCall! And Sabertooth!

"My name's Tomás," he said as they started off.

"Pleased to know you, Tomás," she said. "Mine's Edith."

They walked and walked down Greenwich Street a long way, and then turned left and walked uphill to Broadway and downhill toward another river. Tomás began to smell the fish.

"That there's the East River," Edith said. "Think you can find your way back home?"

"Oh yes!" Tomás said. "I am sure I can." He had a good sense of direction.

All the fish stores were closed. Edith looked in the clean pine boxes standing on the sidewalks, but the boxes held only heads and tails and skeletons of fish.

"Come on," Edith said. "We go see if we can find this man that wanted cabbage."

They found a little, wrinkled, dark man on the splintery wooden pier where the fishing boats docked. He was sitting beside four baskets of fish.

Along the edge of the pier and on the corrugated

tin roofs, seagulls stood. They were the biggest gulls Tomás had ever seen. On their spindly legs they looked twice as big as McCall. The white ones with yellow bills looked clean and neat. The gray ones looked scruffy, like city pigeons. Tomás wanted to shout and run at them to make them fly, but he was afraid to. They looked as though they might turn on him.

Edith put two cabbages and a bunch of bananas on the box beside the man, who immediately took fish from the baskets and laid them on newspaper. Each fish was about the size of the man's hand.

"This is Tomás," Edith said.

The man said, "Pleased to know you," and counted out twelve more fish onto another newspaper. Tomás offered his peppers in return. The man accepted two.

Walking back toward the subway, Edith said, "He works there, making boxes. He takes the rest of the fish up to Harlem later and sells 'em.

"That's where I'm going now," she added, stopping before the subway entrance. "Sure hope I see you around again. I got a grandson your age. Remember, Friday's the best day for fish, but Monday, Tuesday and Wednesday, they good, too."

" 'Bye, Edith. And thank you!" Tomás shouted. He hurried home, holding fast to the loosely wrapped newspaper package, and smiling over the thought of the unexpected feast he was bringing to Fernanda.

9

TRAPPED

On Friday morning Tomás woke to the sound of long-drawn hoots. Foghorns! The boats sounded lost.

Remembering he had a lot to do because it was Friday, he dressed and skipped into the kitchen. Fernanda was washing her face at the sink. He was surprised to see that the world outside the windows was gray and misty.

He took his turn at the sink. Fernanda spooned coffee into his cup and poured in hot water.

"I bet it's late," he worried. "I better hurry."

The foghorns called and called. *Bleep! Moo-oo-oo!* Toot-toot! . . . Groan! . . . Moan! . . . Rowr!

"They sound like a traffic jam calling for help!" Tomás laughed.

He gulped the last swallow of coffee, shouted good-bye, and sprang up the ladder. No need to worry about anyone seeing him this morning. He could hardly see from one roof to the next, the fog was so thick. It was like walking in a cloud.

When he reached the roof door of the Pérez's building, he received a surprise. The door did not open. He tried again. It was *locked*—locked on the inside. He remembered the big hook that had always dangled there. It took him no time at all to realize the spot he was in.

If he could open the door a crack, he thought, he could slide in a wire and raise the hook.

But the door fitted tightly. He braced himself and tugged, hoping the dry wood might give. Nothing happened.

He wanted to haul back and kick the door, but the tin would make a booming sound. Someone might come and ask what he was doing there.

I have to get downstairs, he thought. I've got to find our food for the weekend. Besides, he did not want to go back and be stuck in the kitchen all day. Staying inside might be all right for Fernanda, but he liked the noise and activity of the street, the loading and shouting and honking followed on Friday afternoon by the gradual clearing-out of everybody, leaving the streets to him.

But food was the important thing. He had not been hungry for a long time, and he did not wish to be again.

He stood looking around at the chimneys and walls lurking in the fog. He noticed the backless chair he had used before. He snapped his fingers. Jumping up on it, he managed to skin up on the next building. It was much higher than the one he had climbed from. He knew there were three other buildings the same height next to it. Their roofs were separated only by low walls. He walked along the back edge of the buildings, looking for a fire escape which came clear to the roof.

On the last roof stood a row of six potted plants. Tomás could not remember having seen them when he had explored here before. He wondered who they belonged to.

He was about to turn back when he thought of trying the door. Perhaps the owner of the plants had forgotten to lock it.

Walking lightly for fear his footsteps would be heard by someone underneath, he went and gave the handle a light tug. The metal door swung out to his grasp with a slight squeal. Though he had hoped it might open, its doing so astonished him. He paused, gathering courage to go downstairs. With luck he could make it to the street without anyone seeing him. If someone did see him, his story was simple: he was visiting his aunt. He had gone up on the roof. Someone had locked him out.

He took a deep breath, pulled the door softly shut behind him, and started down the dim stairway. At the foot of it there was another door. His heart sank. *That* one would be locked.

He turned the handle, expecting, if it opened, to find a hallway. What he saw made him close the door quickly. This was not another empty building. Some-one *lived* there. He opened it a crack to take a better look.

The room looked like a room from the magazines— *really* like one. It was big—almost the length of the building, with a skylight in the ceiling. In the long side wall was a fireplace filled with white flowers and dark green leaves. Not plastic flowers like Mrs. Malloy's. Real ones. He could see fallen petals on the deep red carpet. Two pink, curly couches faced each other across a low table on which sat a milkwhite bowl piled high with red apples, round pink radishes and long white ones.

Tomás stood, fascinated. His eyes went from the pictures on the walls to the plants and small trees planted in wooden tubs near the front windows. On the window sill sat a monkey-faced cat—a cat with big ears and bright blue eyes.

Tomás tiptoed along the wall toward a door that he thought must lead to the next flight of stairs. He put his hand on the doorknob, then paused for one more look around. Nearby was an archway. Whatever was behind it was closed off by shutter-doors. He hesitated. There was no sound anywhere. The muffling fog gave him a sense of being the only person in the whole build-ing, in the entire Market.

He walked swiftly to the shutter-doors and opened them an inch. He stepped in to get a better look. At first he thought the room was empty. Then he saw that the walls were hung with drawings of a boy—a boy fishing, a boy in a coonskin cap, a boy milking a cow. The pictures were pinned every which way, some on top of each other.

The cat followed him in and watched Tomás. It did not seem unfriendly, but Tomás did not speak to it.

The floor was bare and splintery and splattered with paint. On a metal-topped kitchen table by one window were fat tubes and little thin tubes, full ones, flattened ones, and some rolled up like empty toothpaste tubes. The center of the table was covered with smears and blobs of paint.

Tomás shook his head. What a mess!

In the far corner stood a wooden thing, something like a ladder, holding a square of stiff white paper which someone had smeared with blue on top and a lot of green in one corner. Two big lights stood near it on tall, thin legs.

He took a last look around. The room was brighter now. Outside the fog was lifting. He could see the shuttered windows of the building across the court. He had better go.

He started for the stairway in high spirits. Maybe he would come back some time. This place was interesting. He wondered who lived here.

He was about to open the door that led downstairs when he heard sounds on the other side. Someone was coming up the stairs and shifting a paper bag from one arm to the other.

"Come on, Omar," a woman's voice said. "Hurry up!"

There was no mistaking the scurry of feet. Omar was a dog.

Tomás stood where he was. It was too late to try to hide.

10

BARBARA RANSOME

The next moment, the door was opened. A lady with a big bag of groceries and a smooth tan dog came in. The dog immediately began to yap at Tomás. He took a step backwards.

"Hello!" the lady shouted above the yapping. "I see the man from the egg store let you in. Omar! Stop it!"

She gave the dog a firm nudge with her sandal, and he went bounding through the room, springing and yapping at the cat. The cat looked at the dog with disdain.

Tomás stood watching, bewildered and a little frightened.

The woman disappeared behind a screen. She put the paper bag down with a thud, and turned on a light.

Tomás thought of bolting out the door and down the stairs. But just then the lady put her head around the screen and asked, "Didn't anybody come with you?"

Tomás shook his head.

"Hungry?" She peeled a banana. "How about a snack before we start?"

She set a glass of orange soda and cookies on a round table beside the screen. "Sit down," she said, seating herself.

Tomás took a quick look at the door by which he had hoped to escape. The silly dog came sniffing at him.

"Don't mind Omar," the lady said.

Tomás sat down on the edge of the chair and took a long drink of soda. Over the rim of the glass he studied the girl.

A band of blue ribbon held her tan-colored hair out

of her eyes. Her eyes were blue and she was wearing a faded blue shirt and tan slacks. Her arms and face and sandaled feet were as brown as his.

"What's your name?" she asked, serious as a teacher.

"Tomás Angelito Lorca."

"Ah, Tomás." She nodded. *Yo me llamo Barbara. Qué edad tienes?* How old are you?"

"Eleven," he said. "You speak Spanish!"

"A little." She pushed the plate toward him. "Have a cookie."

He took one of the three thick, chocolate-covered cookies. He wanted to eat slowly, feeling his teeth sink through the layer of chocolate into marshmallow, but he dared not. As soon as she found out how he came to be here, she would throw him out and maybe call the police. He chewed rapidly, stuffing the last bite into his mouth with his left hand while he reached for the second cookie with his right.

"Don't choke," she cautioned. "I'm not in that much of a hurry. Did you come here all by yourself, or did someone bring you?"

He swallowed, washed down the cookie with a drink of soda, and said:

"The man from the egg store didn't let me up—" He watched her, alert for a scowl. "I came across the roof."

Her eyebrows arched. "The roof?" Not anger but curiosity was in her voice.

"I was visiting my aunt. In the other building." He

pointed. "I went up on the roof and somebody locked me out."

Her blue eyes opened a little wider, but she didn't sound excited. She hardly sounded interested. "Then you're not the child from the agency?"

He shook his head slowly, wishing he were.

"Good thing my door was open," she said. She glanced at a big clock on the wall. "Where is that boy?"

Tomás shrugged, and smiled a little wistfully.

"Never mind him," she said. "What are we going to do about you?"

"That's no trouble," he assured her. "All I have to do is go downstairs, and then up the stairs to my aunt's."

"I see." Barbara nodded. "I didn't know any children lived in the neighborhood." She gestured toward the last cookie. "You better have that before you go. Do you live with your aunt?"

He didn't want to say yes and he didn't want to say no, so he said, "Sometimes."

Barbara looked at the clock again. "If the other boy doesn't come, would you like to pose for me?"

Tomás looked puzzled. "Yes," he said, "but I don't know if I know how."

"I draw pictures—pictures for children's books."

Tomás nodded, but she saw that he still did not understand.

"You know—for books like the ones you have in school and in the library," she said.

She went to a bookcase and took out a thin, green-covered book. Opening it, she showed him a picture of a Chinese boy sailing a kite. Tomás remembered seeing a picture like it pinned to the wall in the bare room. He ran his hand over the page.

She closed the book and showed him the front cover. One line read *Pictures by Barbara Ransome.*

Tomás gave her a pleased look. "You want to draw pictures of me? They'd be in a book?"

"Yes."

"Does—" he faltered. "Does it cost anything?"

"Cost you?"

"Like a camera picture," he explained.

"No—" She turned to put the book away. "No, this is different. I pay you."

"Wow!" He jumped up, becoming alert and businesslike.

"It's hard work," she cautioned.

"I like hard work," he bragged, giving himself a brisk slap on the chest.

She looked at the clock again. "Can you come back this afternoon? I should certainly know by then whether the other boy is coming. If he does, I'll let you pose for me another day."

Tomás nodded and started for the door. With all the excitement, he had forgotten the many things he had to do—remove the hook at the top of the stairs, find food, and sneak in some more kerosene.

Barbara Ransome said, "Come back by way of the roof, if you want, or ring the doorbell downstairs."

"Okay!" He jumped noisily down the stairs, two at a time, all the way to the sidewalk. He could not believe he could be so lucky. That woman was going to pay him to draw his picture. It might even be in a schoolbook, though he could not imagine how this could be.

But if nothing else came of meeting Barbara Ransome, he would have two ways to come and go from the hideout—like some little animals that he had read about. They lived in the ground and had two or three holes to get in and out by. That's how it would be with him now.

He was so happy he began to run and to sing Mr. Malloy's favorite song:

If her eyes are blue as skies,
That's Peggy O'Neil.
If she's smiling all the while,
That's Peggy O'Neil . . .

Then he whistled the tune as he raced from one box of discarded vegetables to another. He'd learned to clean the vegetables with a pocket knife he had found in a junk pile. It made less food to carry upstairs and less garbage to carry down.

When he had enough vegetables and fruit, he bought kerosene at the service station and put the jug into a purple mesh bag. A gallon lasted a long time—more than a week.

Finally, he climbed the four flights of steps and un-hooked the door. The sun was shining now and already the roof felt hot. No air stirred, not even up here.

He set the food and kerosene in the shade of the wall and set about unscrewing the big hook with his pocket knife. When it came loose, he stood holding it, wondering where to put it. It wasn't his, so he didn't feel right about throwing it away. At last he fastened it to a rusty TV antenna. No one, he said to himself, would trouble to put it back.

He scuttled over the wall and home.

Breathlessly, he told Fernanda about the locked door, about the unlocked door on the other roof, and the beautiful room. She made him describe the beauti-ful room twice.

"What a nice lady," he bubbled, waving his hands. "She's tall like a movie star and wears pants. And she's going to draw pictures of me. She puts them in books."

Fernanda looked wistful.

"If you'd go outside, you could come with me," Tomás suggested slyly.

"Maybe, someday," she said.

She had cooked rice with pimientos and tomatoes again.

"When are you going to get more fish?" she asked.

"Maybe today, if I have time. Wow, am I busy!" He counted on his fingers. "Go get fish. See if Mrs. Salvador or Mrs. Pérez wants a baby-sitter. Go work for that lady—I hope! Whew! I never worked so hard in my life." He drank off the juice left in his bowl. "Pretty soon, I'll buy us some meat."

Then he remembered the third chocolate-covered cookie still in his pocket. He hauled it out, crumpled and melting, and handed it to Fernanda.

"Is she nice—the Señora?" Fernanda asked, licking the chocolate with the tip of her tongue.

"I told you she was," he said.

"Pretty?"

Fernanda always asked such girl questions.

"So long, I got things to do," he said and stepped out onto the fire escape.

On the roof he kept a wary eye out for the watchman. Across the river, flat blue now, the huge clock said twelve. The fire siren down the street gave its noon wail.

No, the Salvadors and the Pérezes did not need him. Perhaps tomorrow.

He set off on the long walk to the Fulton Fish Market.

11

BARBARA TAKES PICTURES

An hour and a half later Tomás stood on the sidewalk before the lady's door. In one arm he held a bundle of fish which he had wrapped in many layers of newspaper. He pressed the bell. Above it a neat card said

Barbara Ransome
ILLUSTRATOR

He heard a faint shout. He stepped back and looked up. She leaned out a window and threw down a tightly-rolled piece of brown paper. It landed on the sidewalk. He picked it up and unrolled it. It became a paper bag with a key inside.

He unlocked the door, and started up the stairs. The lower floors were dusty and empty. She's like us, he thought. She lives in an empty building. She has a hide-out, too, because nobody could ever find her unless she wanted them to.

She was waiting at the top of the stairs. Omar yapped

twice, ran away, and came skittering back to sniff at Tomás's feet.

"Miss—" Tomás began, "Miss, did the boy come?"

"No, he didn't. You have the job."

Tomás gave her a wide smile.

"You can call me Barbara," she said. "What have you got there?"

"Fish," he said shyly. "You can have some."

"How nice! Thank you. What kind of fish?"

"Just *fish* fish, I guess." He began to unwrap it.

"Looks good," she said. She picked up a round, meaty chunk. "This is about enough for me and the cat. How much was it?"

At that moment the cat purred and rubbed against Tomás's leg. "Mrowr?" the cat asked.

"This is Owa," Barbara said. "He smells the fish."

"I never saw a cat like him," Tomás confessed.

"He's a Siamese cat. Aren't you, Owa?" She looked seriously at Tomás. "His full name in Siamese is Owa-Taygoo-Siam. Can you say that—fast?"

Tomás shrugged. "Owa Taygoo Siam," he said easily. Then he heard the words come back to him: *Oh, what a goose I am!* He began to laugh.

He told her about Sabertooth and McCall. After a name like Owa, McCall did not seem so crazy.

"How much was the fish?" Barbara asked again.

"It was free," he explained. "Over at the fish market they just put it on the sidewalk for people to take."

100

"The *Fulton* Fish Market? Have you been clear over there and back?"

"Yes."

"Suppose I put it all in the icebox for now—till you're ready to leave. I'll take some as a gift today, but after this you'll have to let me pay you."

"All right," Tomás said. "Maybe I could sell some to other people, too."

She agreed and then said, "Come on in the studio. Let's get to work." She went into the room with the pictures hanging every which way on the walls. Tomás followed. A camera lay on the table.

"I'm going to be drawing pictures of a farm boy," she explained. "So I'll take pictures of you, sitting or standing the way I tell you. Then I draw from the snapshots. That way you don't have to sit in one position for hours at a time.

She took a pair of faded blue overalls from one of the shelves. Handing them to him, she said, "Go in the other room and put these on. Take off your T-shirt and your shoes. I want you wearing just the overalls."

Tomás giggled with embarrassment, but he obeyed. The dog trotted after him.

Tomás peeled off his shirt and twitched it at Omar. "Hey, boy," he whispered.

With a joyous growl Omar sank his teeth into the shirt and pulled. Tomás, a little surprised and frightened, pulled, too. Something ripped. He loosed his

hold, and Omar raced off with the shirt to the front of the room.

Tomás stood wondering what to do. He had never owned a dog. He had never even known a dog. Omar was small, but his teeth looked sharp.

"Miss! I mean, Barbara!" he shouted. "Omar stole my shirt."

"Go get it," she called. "Hurry up. I'm about ready."

Tomás started, then stopped, standing on one foot.

"I'm scared he'll bite me."

"Omar? He only bites old men."

Tomás had to laugh. He ran to the front of the room. Omar lay crouched over the shirt. He growled.

Tomás stopped in his tracks. "He's growling," he reported.

"Growl back!"

Tomás bent forward and snarled.

Leaving the shirt, Omar bounded toward him, barking. Tomás dodged around a chair. Omar followed. Tomás dived for the shirt, whipping it away just before Omar's teeth snapped together on empty air.

"I got it," he shouted, laughing, running back to the chair where the other clothes lay.

Omar, panting, watched him pull on the faded overalls.

These are crazy pants, Tomás thought. He had seen them in books and on TV. They were what you wore in the country.

He found Barbara waiting with the camera. She looked him over. "You'll do, I think. Get up on the platform. Sit down and relax while I fix the lights."

She brought the tall lights on legs and stood them in the middle of the floor and turned them on him. They were too bright to look at.

"All right." She stood in the middle of the room,

looking at him. "Pretend you're a farm boy. You're lying on your stomach in the grass."

Tomás obediently rolled on his stomach.

"No, not sleeping," she directed. "Hold your head up."

Tomás raised his head.

"Have you ever been to Central Park? Ever lain in the grass?" she asked.

"No!" Tomás giggled at the thought of such foolishness. "A bee might sting me." He squinted, trying to see her beyond the bright lights. "I could be lying on the roof, though, looking at the river."

"Do that. Fine! Stay that way."

He heard a click.

"Okay," she said. "Remember how you were lying. I want to get another picture in a minute." She began to count: "—three, four—" At the count of ten she opened a door in the back of the camera and ripped out a piece of paper. She looked at it closely and then handed it to Tomás.

"Hey!" he cried. "That's me!"

It was the first picture he'd seen of himself since he was a baby, not counting a class picture in which his head had been a blur the size of a pencil eraser.

"Let me have it a minute," Barbara said. "We have to coat it with this stuff or it will fade." She showed him a round metal tube with a felt strip down the side. She rubbed the felt over the picture, turning it shiny. "There, see? Now, it'll keep."

He went back to lying on his stomach, pretending to watch boats on the river. Then she had him sit cross-legged, with one arm around Omar. She took more pictures. She let him coat each picture as it came out of the camera until, thinking of Fernanda, he could not help exclaiming, "I wish I could have one!"

"You can. But not any of these. I need these to work from. I'll take one later that will be just for you. Right now, I want you to stand on one foot. Pretend you're walking along a narrow railing." She drew a chalk line across the platform. "There, that's the fence."

Tomás had to do it again and again. He began to sweat. "The lights are so hot!" he complained.

"I know." She pushed back a lock of hair from her own damp forehead. "But we have to have them. If it's not light, the camera can't see. I told you it was work."

"Yeah." He nodded wearily. "I don't mind," he added, stretching out along the edge òf the platform while she waited for the picture to develop itself. "I like to work. When I grow up, I'm going to work all the time."

"If you work as well as you do now, you'll be rich."

"I will?" Tomás sat up, giving her all his attention.

"*I* think so," Barbara was saying.

"You think I work good now?" he asked, wanting to be sure.

"Yes," she said, not looking up from putting a new film pack into the camera.

Tomás jumped up and ran to look out the open window to hide how pleased he felt. Outside he could not see far. The air was like mist, but hot and sticky.

"All right," she said. "That's enough for today. We've been working two hours."

Tomás leaned on the table, studying each picture again and again.

"Here," Barbara said, picking one out of the group. "This one's for you."

The picture, taken close up, showed his head and shoulders. His hair looked thick and black; his dark eyes, bright as a puppy's.

"Will you need it to draw from?" he asked worriedly.

"If I do, I'll borrow it back."

At the little table next to the kitchen they drank Cokes and ate more cookies. Tomás leaned back in his chair, letting his legs dangle.

"Did you live here last month?" he asked remembering the plants on the roof, which had not been there before.

She told him she had been visiting in Mexico for half a year.

"Who lived here then?"

"A friend of mine."

Crossing his fingers under the table, he asked the question he was afraid to ask: "Are you going to live here now?"

"Yes."

He leaned forward, set his soda bottle on the table, and leaned back again. "I'm glad." He smiled.

"Do you like it here?" he asked, thinking what a silly question that was. How could anyone not like it—with a dog and all these colors and a whole roof of your own.

"I like it all right," she said.

Tomás looked around the pretty room. One thing was missing. "Don't you have a TV?" he asked.

"No," she said, and he could tell from her voice that she did not want one.

"I'll pay you now." She was getting her purse from the kitchen. "I'm going to visit my brother. I haven't seen him since I got back."

She returned with a brown billfold. "Two hours . . . two dollars."

Tomás could scarcely believe his ears, but it was true. She was handing him two green bills.

"Gee," he shouted. "Wow! Thanks!" He started for the stairway to the roof.

"Hey, your fish! And your picture," she called.

He rushed back. He put the money deep in his pocket, took the wrapped fish in one hand and the photo in the other. He ran through the living room to the door, and turned to shout goodbye. She was still standing by the table.

She took a step forward. "Stop by next week—"

"Okay!" he called happily.

He shut the door after him and ran up the stairs. The roof door on its heavy spring slammed behind him. Slowly, cautiously, he went from roof to roof, one eye cocked for the watchman. The docks and the river had their Friday evening look, the Market, its Friday quiet. Perhaps *this* was the weekend Papa would come.

Meantime, he could hardly wait to show Fernanda the picture and the money.

12

FINDING THINGS

As often as he could find an excuse, Tomás visited
Barbara. The long busy days lost themselves in one
another. He and Fernanda ate less rice, more fresh
vegetables. The fish, the vegetables and fruit, the
cracked eggs and frankfurters he bought, all began
to make a difference in the way the children looked.
The sun in the back room helped, too. Fernanda's
cheeks and lips turned pink. Her black eyes sparkled.

Tomás found more things to please her. One day he
found a white saucepan with a red handle, only a little
bit chipped. It delighted Fernanda. Another day, in
Staple Street, he found a teakettle.

"It was just sitting in a doorway," he told her. "It
probably leaks."

But it did not leak. Fernanda rubbed it till it shone.

From the dump up the street, he brought a chair one
day, and a small table the next.

Fernanda still had some of the yellow silk material.
She cut it into curtains to hang over the tin-covered
windows in the cave room.

Tomás bought kerosene and candles and candy and oleo and eggs and coffee and soap, and even bread once in a while.

Everywhere he found things. He or Fernanda had only to wish for something, it seemed, and within a few days he would come across it, dumped somewhere, waiting for him. At times he almost thought they did have a godmother, a fairy godmother, but that was crazy—a story for second graders.

One day Fernanda glanced up from her scrapbook. "Look, here is a room with yellow curtains, just like ours." She studied the colored photograph. "These people have a big picture hanging between the yellow curtains."

"Barbara has big pictures on her walls," Tomás bragged. "Here—and here—and here!" He ran around the cave room, pointing, showing Fernanda where Barbara would have pictures if this were her room. "—and over the fireplace."

"We need a picture," Fernanda said.

Tomás leaned against the wall. "It's pretty dark in here for a picture."

Instead of replying, Fernanda walked to the wall where she wanted to hang the picture. She stood on tiptoe and reached as high as she could. "Look," she said, "there's a nail already in the wall."

Tomás dropped his shoulders. "I'll try."

Three days later he saw something square leaning

against an empty wooden cheese barrel. He went closer to see what it was and could hardly believe his eyes. It was a picture. A big one, with frame and glass and a wire to hang it by. He squatted down to look at it more closely. He wiped off some of the dirt. The glass wasn't the least bit cracked. Under the glass was a white cardboard frame, and inside that a brown one, and inside that—He rubbed more dirt away and saw a familiar face.

George Washington!

He clutched it quickly to him so that the two men who were passing should not see it. If they saw whose picture it was, they might take it away. He stole a look at the nearest doorways. But no, someone had put it carefully there for anyone who wanted it.

Tomás hid his basket of vegetables behind the big wooden barrel. Then he picked up George Washington, carried him in both arms, watching every step he took.

When at last he got the picture safely down the fire escape into the house, and on the table in front of Fernanda, he drew a deep breath. His arms ached, but he had brought it home without damaging it at all.

Fernanda liked the picture, especially its size and the white lacy scarf George Washington was wearing around his neck.

"Was this his market?" she asked, washing the glass.

Tomás was scornful. "He was a President. He didn't bother with markets."

Fernanda stood on a box and hooked the wire hanger over the nail, while Tomás stood back and made sure it hung straight.

Fernanda did not seem surprised that Tomás had found the picture. Tomás wondered if she thought the streets were filled with good things, there for the taking. Well, they were, of course. But there's work to it, too, he said to himself, going back downstairs to fetch the vegetables.

He went past the same spot again the next morning just for luck and saw something else on the loading dock—a long, dusty roll of paper, standing on end. He jumped up on the dock and unrolled it part way—far enough to see that it was a map.

Like at school, he thought excitedly. And like the school maps, it was fastened to round, black sticks at the top and bottom. He unrolled it a little more, cocked his head sideways, and read the row of square letters across the top, UNION PACIFIC RAILROAD. On one side it said, *Geographically correct map of the United States.* His heart gave a jump of excitement. I can teach Fernanda, he thought.

Quickly he re-rolled it, tucked it under his arm, and marched home. When you found a special treasure the first thing to do was to get it safely home. Otherwise somebody else might take it.

He found Fernanda elbow-deep in suds, washing one of her dresses and two of his T-shirts.

113

"Look," he called gleefully from the fire escape. "Look what I found today!"

"What?" She left the sink and stood watching while he put the roll on the clean-swept floor.

"A map!" He looked around for something heavy enough to hold the top end flat while he unrolled it.

"Wait, I know." Fernanda ran into the other room and returned with two bricks.

In his eagerness to see the whole thing Tomás unrolled the old paper too hastily. One edge began to tear away from the top stick.

"*Cuidado!*" Fernanda warned. "Careful! It's tearing."

The brittle, browned paper had already cracked in several places.

"Oh!" Tomás mourned. Kneeling, he fitted the crumbled edges together as if, put back in place, some magic would mend them.

"Never mind," Fernanda said soothingly. "I'll patch it on the back with paste and strips of paper. What's it a map of?" She walked around to where she could look down at some letters. "Gulf—of—Mex—" she began to read.

"Gulf of Mexico!" Tomás shouted. "It's a map of the United States. See, here's every state."

"Where's New York?"

"Here. See, here's where we are." He crawled back and forth. In the bottom corners smaller maps were set

114

in. He crouched on knees and elbows, chin in hand. " 'Atlantic Ocean and Principal Steamship Lines between Atlantic Ocean Ports,' " he read aloud. "Oh, boy! Here's where all those ships come from. Across there—" His finger followed dotted lines across the blue ocean between the continents and then moved quickly to the western corner, and to the Pacific.

"Where's Puerto Rico?" Fernanda asked.

"I know. Wait a minute." Tomás searched the small map of the Atlantic Ocean. "Cuba . . . Haiti . . . here—Puerto Rico."

"So small?"

"This is just a small map."

Sabertooth joined them. He walked curiously across the paper, sniffing, plopped down on the Great Lakes and licked his side.

"A monster!" Tomás cried, falling over backwards. "A monster is prowling across the country . . . from west to east. When, ladies and gentlemen, he gets to New York City, stay in your apartments. One lash of his tail will kill a thousand people!"

"One scratch of his claw will tear the map, too," Fernanda said matter-of-factly.

Tomás swooped up the cat. "Come on, Monster. You have to go back to Mars."

Together, Tomás and Fernanda mended the map and hung it on the wall above the table where they could study it during meals.

One hot, muggy Sunday two men cleaned out a whole building on Duane Street. They were dumping the last odds and ends on the sidewalk when Tomás rounded the corner. He watched them finish up and lock the door. He stood wide-eyed as they climbed into their car and drove away.

For a moment he couldn't move. Here was unbelievable treasure. It was so splendid he was unable to decide where to dig first. He walked around the edge. There was a brown leather couch, but it was so old the leather was crumbling to dust. It sent up a brown powder even when you touched it gently. There were two office desks but they were in pieces. Most of the boxes were filled with stacks of gray cardboard, dividers for egg cartons. They were spotted with yolk and bits of broken egg shell.

Next he came across a man's tan raincoat, with a big label inside that gave washing instructions. It had no rips; he laid it aside.

He dug in further, and found some books, which delighted him until he saw that the pages were covered with black squiggles instead of words. He laid one aside so that he could ask someone what it meant. He found some pads of blank paper and four unsharpened pencils, and then, opening a neat cardboard box, he came across a folded pink washcloth which looked and felt brand new. Underneath it lay a heavy paper-wrapped package. He tore open the wrapping.

116

It was a bolt of cloth. The pink roses and green leaves on a white background were so beautiful that he gave a low whistle. His eyes sparkled. What Fernanda could do with that! He unfolded a little of the cloth. There seemed to be yards of it. It was a good thing that Grandmama had taught Fernanda to sew.

"She can make herself about sixty dresses," he said.

With his usual caution he gathered up this treasure, put the cloth back in the box along with the pads, the pencils, the washcloth and the raincoat, and hurried home.

Until he reached the roof with his prizes he had been too busy to notice the dark clouds settling in low over the city. A spatter of rain fell as he made the fire-escape landing. While he was unpacking the box, it began to rain hard.

He and Fernanda lit a candle and sat looking at Tomás's marvelous finds and listening to the rain. Fernanda made a jar of lemonade from a lime and two lemons Tomás had found on Friday, and as they drank it, they talked about what Fernanda could make from the cloth of roses. A dress, of course. Maybe two. She could see herself in them. They would be beautiful.

"Oh dear!" she suddenly cried in dismay.

"What?" Tomás demanded.

"I have the needle, but I used up all the thread to make the curtains."

"That is nothing, Fernanda." Tomás waved his hand. "I will buy you some tomorrow."

"There is enough cloth for our whole family." She giggled. "I can make a dress for McCall and a tiny shirt for Sabertooth," she added as Sabertooth made a dive under a fold of the cloth.

"Would you like that?" she demanded of the kitten, pulling him out and holding him at arm's length above her head.

"I have an idea!" Tomás shouted. "Why don't you make something for Barbara?"

Fernanda stared at him, thrilled with the idea. "What could I make?" she asked slowly.

"A dress?"

"I don't know how big she is."

"A tablecloth, then."

Fernanda shook her head.

"A handkerchief!"

"No, silly." Fernanda took a sip of lemonade and put her chin in her hand. "I could make an apron, a pretty apron . . . with a ruffle. Look, I saw one in the new magazine. I'll show you."

She found the picture and shoved it under Tomás's nose.

"Could you make that?" he asked, impressed.

She nodded.

"Yes? Do it then. Maybe she'll like it so much, she'll let you come over and look at her house."

Fernanda sighed. "I'd like to see it."

"Oh, you'd like it, Fernanda," Tomás said. "It's

118

prettier than all those pictures together, because you can walk around and smell it and feel the pink couches, or touch anything you want to."

He looked at her from the corner of his eye.

Fernanda reached for one of the scrapbooks which happened to be lying on the table. She opened it. "I can walk around these rooms, too," she said, fingering the pictures. Her face took on a stubborn look.

Tomás wanted to shout, "You can NOT!" but he caught himself and stopped. Instead, he took the magazine with the apron picture and laid it on top of the open scrapbook.

"How soon could you make the apron?" he asked.

Fernanda thought for a moment. "Three days, maybe more."

"Would you go to Barbara's then—if she'd let you?"

Fernanda studied the picture of the apron. "I might."

Tomás sat on the floor beside all the good things. He swallowed the last of his lemonade and rocked back and forth, hugging himself. "Isn't it nice here? Haven't you had more fun since we've lived here, Fernanda?"

A shadow crossed her face, but she answered readily enough, *"Sí."*

However, when they sat down to supper that night, she picked up her fork and laid it down again. "Tomás, we have been here a long time."

"Yes," Tomás agreed. He had no idea how long. It is hard to keep track of time without a calendar. Without school to tell him the day of the week, he had trouble enough knowing when Friday came round. Whether it was July or August made little difference. He supposed he would somehow know when school reopened.

"So what?" he asked finally.

"I do not think Papa is coming back."

Tomás felt a pain in the middle of his chest. It hurt so much for a minute that he could not speak. Then it went away, leaving him very sad. He missed Papa. Papa had sung a lot whenever he was home. Tomás felt so sad that the food made a lump in his throat, but he did not feel afraid.

"I will look out for us," he said. "Barbara says I work so hard that when I grow up, I will be rich." A sudden fear struck him. "Fernanda, don't you like it here?"

"*Si,* Tomasito. But we cannot *stay* here."

"Why not?"

"Winter will come. How will we keep warm?"

Tomás leaned back in the chair. "I'll think of something," he promised.

13

RAIN

As if to prove Fernanda's words, the next day the weather turned cool. As Tomás went about his chores, the problem settled in the back of his mind and bothered him: Papa is not coming back. What are we going to do?

For three days it rained. Fernanda cut off the bottom of the raincoat and shortened the sleeves. When Tomás wore it he fancied he looked like a spy on TV. Between downpours the sky stayed gray, the air damp. It seemed to him that summer had lasted a long while. It must be nearly school time. He went to ask Barbara.

"How did you know I wanted you?" she exclaimed when she opened the roof door.

"You want me to pose again?" he asked, pleased that he remembered the word.

"This time you're going to be a Puerto Rican boy— just like you. Except the boy in this story has just come to New York."

"I've never been to Puerto Rico," Tomás said.

"I haven't either," Barbara said. "But I may go there this winter. Come on in. I'll show you the pictures I drew of you."

As they went downstairs a wonderful idea struck Tomás. "Maybe I'll go, too!" He remembered a sign he'd passed on the way to school: *PUERTO RICO and back, $13.00.* "How much do you think it would cost to just *go* there?" he asked.

"About a hundred dollars," Barbara said. "Maybe a little less."

"A hundred dollars! No—" He told her about the sign.

When she explained that $13 was the down payment, and that you had to come back and pay the rest of the money, Tomás was stunned. But he didn't give up the idea entirely. It was still a good one. The problem was how.

Perhaps Barbara would take him along to pose. No, there were probably a thousand boys in Puerto Rico who would be glad to pose.

"Miss . . ." he began. "I mean, Barbara, is the summer over?"

"Looks like it, doesn't it?" she said cheerfully.

"I mean, is it time for school to start?"

She glanced at a calendar on the wall. "No, you have a whole month yet. Don't worry, it'll get hot again."

The picture she showed him was of a boy not wearing shoes.

"Doesn't he cut his feet, walking barefoot like that?" Tomás asked.

"Sometimes," she said, "but he doesn't mind. There —see—he's wearing a Band-Aid."

Then she took pictures of Tomás pretending to chase a chicken, and cutting sugar cane with a long knife.

After they had both worked hard for a long time, she put the camera away. "I have to show a boy swimming, too," she said. "I guess we should go to the beach for that." She looked at him, and the way she asked, "Do you like the beach?" made him feel she was teasing him.

"I don't know," he confessed.

Her eyes widened. "Haven't you ever been swimming?"

"Yes, a long time ago. When Raimundo and his sister lived here, we went sometimes to the pool at Carmine Street."

"I guess we'd better take you to the beach, then."

"When?"

"Not today. It's supposed to rain again. How about next week?"

"Yes!" He spun around on one heel. "Oh!" His face fell. "I don't have a bathing suit any more."

"We can fix that," she said, and looked up as raindrops pelted against the skylight.

"You'd better wait here till it stops," she told him. "You don't want to get wet. Besides, you might slip on the roof and fall."

Tomás agreed to wait.

Barbara gave him a peanut butter and jelly sandwich, a glass of milk, and a book to read. She ate while she worked at her drawing board.

She had put down an old rug under the window where he could lie while he read and ate. He pretended it was a raft. Omar swam across the floor to join him. Tomás pulled him aboard. Owa the Siamese found a sheet of drawing paper and curled himself up on a raft of his own.

Before anyone noticed, the afternoon was over. Again Barbara paid him two dollars. She also let him borrow the book.

After dark, back in their cave room, Tomás built a fire and read Fernanda the story by candlelight. Rain drummed against the tin-covered windows. A few drops fell down the chimney to sizzle on the coals. McCall crouched by the fireplace and Sabertooth curled in Fernanda's lap. They felt very snug.

Next morning, clouds still hung low. Tomás went to see Barbara first thing. He found her on the roof, sitting on a stool, with a large drawing board on her knees. Omar saw him, barked, and then ran to him to be petted. Tomás picked him up, hugged him, and gave Barbara a big smile.

"Hello, Tomás."

She was drawing the gray, oily river, the gray, curly clouds, the black buildings along the edge.

He shivered, and wished the sun would shine. "When are you going to Puerto Rico?" he asked.

"Oh, not for a long time," she answered, keeping her eyes on her pencil. "Don't worry, we'll go to the beach first."

"Will your brother go to Puerto Rico, too?"

She glanced at him. "How did you know about my brother?"

"You were going to visit him one day."

125

"So I was. No, he's too busy."

"Does he draw pictures, too?"

She shook her head. "No, he's a doctor. A special doctor—a psychiatrist. People go to him if they feel unhappy or afraid, and he helps them."

"Afraid?"

"Well, yes, afraid of things they shouldn't be afraid of. Things most people aren't afraid of."

"Like the Market watchman? *People* aren't afraid of him—but I am."

She did not look up from the drawing board. "Not quite like that. Maybe you have reason to be afraid of him—"

"He doesn't like me," Tomás said with a shrug.

"Anyhow, that's not the kind of fear I mean. I mean people whose fears keep them from living a normal happy life. You probably don't even know anyone like that."

Tomás did not answer. He was thinking of Fernanda. Perhaps that was the kind of being afraid that Barbara meant.

He said, "Like if somebody was afraid to go outside and never went out of their apartment?"

"Yes." She looked at him in surprise. "Do you know someone like that?"

"Yes. Someone. How could your brother help them?"

"Well, it would depend—on how old the person was,

and on other things. Who do you know who's afraid to go out?"

"This girl. She's fourteen. Could he make her not be afraid to go outside?"

She thought a minute and then said, "My brother's coming for lunch tomorrow. You could ask him."

Tomás looked to see if she meant it, and decided she did. He hugged himself suddenly and rolled his eyes. "I'd be scared to talk to him!"

"Tomás . . . do you realize we've been friends for three weeks, and I don't know the first thing about you —where you live, how many brothers and sisters you have."

"I live with my aunt."

"I thought you were just visiting."

"I live there this summer."

"Who's the girl who's afraid to go out?" Barbara asked.

"Just a girl."

"Has a doctor ever been to see her? An ordinary doctor?"

Tomás shook his head. "She isn't sick."

Barbara said, "You'd better have lunch with us tomorrow and talk to my brother."

Tomás drew a deep breath. "Okay." For Fernanda he would do it.

14

A TRIP TO THE BEACH

Next morning the sun was already hot when Tomás crossed the roof. The city steamed. He could barely see the Statue of Liberty.

"Hi, Tomás," Barbara greeted him. "My brother just called. He's not coming today. Let's go to the beach."

The beach! And not to have to talk to the doctor. He felt doubly glad.

"Go ask your aunt." Tomás started off. "And hurry. It's a long drive."

"Drive?" he echoed. He felt his smile stretching. "Do you have a car?"

"You'll like my car," she promised. "Go ask and hurry back. Tell her I'm taking you to Far Rockaway."

He ran first to tell Fernanda. "I'm going to the beach," he shouted, jumping in through the fire-escape window.

"Where?"

"The beach! It's called Far Rockaway."

Fernanda's eyes widened with fear. "When will you come back?"

"Tonight, silly! I'm going with Barbara. In a car. Goodbye! I have to hurry." He scrambled out the window again, but before climbing the ladder he turned and put his head back into the room. "I'll bring you something nice, Fernanda," he promised. "Maybe candy."

He clambered up the ladder, ran across the roofs, and tiptoed down the stairs to the Pérez apartment. He knocked on the door.

He wished he had never taken up baby-sitting. He visited Mrs. Pérez and Mrs. Salvador every morning, but he worried that one day one of them would go to his old building, looking for him. If that happened, Mrs. Malloy would tell Mr. Malloy, "Tomás is not in Brooklyn. We must get to the bottom of this." And she would.

"I cannot baby-sit today," he said when Mrs. Pérez opened the door. "I am going to the beach."

"*Sí,* that is nice. I will tell Mrs. Salvador. Have a good time."

He ran on down the stairs, his sneakers just touching the edges. He went to Barbara's street door and rang the bell.

She opened the window. "In a minute," she shouted.

She came down carrying a basket and a blue bag with white rope handles. The camera in its brown case was swinging from a strap around her neck.

She had tied a red-and-white bandanna over her hair.

She was wearing a red-and-white shirt to match, and white shorts and sandals.

"You look just like a magazine!" Tomás shouted.

A man walking past turned and winked at him.

When Tomás looked back at Barbara, he saw a dimple disappearing in her cheek.

She handed him the blue bag. "This way." She started off up the street, and Tomás had to run to catch up.

When they passed his old apartment house, he held his breath. Mrs. Malloy might be looking out the window. He tried to walk close beside Barbara so that anyone seeing them would think he was her little boy. He saw no one, but he felt better when a truck that was backed on the sidewalk hid them from view.

Outside the garage in the next block they had to wait while a man brought the car down on an elevator. It was a bright red car with no top.

"That's it," Barbara said.

"Honest? I get to ride in that? Yippee!" He spun around on his heel.

Barbara put the basket, the blue bag, and the camera on the back seat. Tomás sat in front beside her. Then they were rolling down Greenwich Street between parked trucks. He leaned back against the red leather seat and looked up at the familiar buildings. His chest swelled. He took a deep breath and tried to sit still, but he was too excited.

Barbara glanced sideways at him. "Like it?"

"It's like a parade!" He laughed, bouncing on the seat. He hoped everyone would see him. Except Mrs. Malloy. He wished Fernanda could see him. He looked up to the roof, wanting to wave.

"The first stop is to get you a swim suit," Barbara said. "I guess Canal Street would be good."

On Canal Street they passed a clothing store. Barbara turned the corner and stopped. "I can't park," she explained. "Too much traffic. Here—" She took two dollars from her billfold. "You pick out some trunks. Ask the clerk your size. I'll stay with the car."

"Okay!" he cried. Clutching the two bills, he ran around the corner and into the store.

A man showed him a stack of swim trunks his size. Tomás chose red ones. He ran back to the counter with them, and jumped from one foot to the other while the clerk wrapped a set of lace curtains for a woman.

"What's your hurry?" the man teased, putting the trunks in a bag. "The beach won't wash away."

Tomás giggled.

"Okay," the man said, "here's your change. I hope the ocean doesn't dry up before you get there."

Back in the car, Barbara took the trunks from the bag and held them against him. "I guess they'll fit."

She put the change back in her purse, and Tomás carefully took the price tag off his trunks.

"We're off!" she said. Tomás thought her voice sounded happy.

"Are you going to swim?" he asked.

"Yes, of course. Aren't you?"

"Do I have to?"

"No. You can play in the sand, or do whatever you like."

"Is there sand?"

"On the beach? Sure. Lots of it. There's sand and lots of people and beach umbrellas and towels and everything you could want—including a basket of food."

Tomás sat in a blissful daze while the car crawled through the traffic. Suddenly they dipped into a tunnel and the air began to smell strange and choking.

"Do you like breathing here?" he shouted above the roar of wind and tires.

"Terrible!" she shouted back.

He tried holding his breath, but the tunnel went on and on. He began to wonder if it ran the whole way. Going to the beach was not so much fun after all.

Suddenly they came up into fresh air and slowed down. The other cars were forming lines leading to toll-collection booths. Barbara moved her car into line too. When their turn came, she handed the tollhouse man a coin.

"Is this the beach?" Tomás asked.

Barbara shook her head. "No. We pay to use the parkway. We're just getting started."

15

FAR ROCKAWAY

They drove and drove, among hundreds of cars. On the other side hundreds more went whizzing by going toward the city. They drove on a highway built above the street and then along the edge of the water. Barbara said that all that smooth water disappearing into the haze was part of New York's harbor.

After a long time she drove into a parking lot. Tomás saw nothing but buildings. "Where's the water?" he asked.

Barbara was taking things out of the car. "Over there," she said, tossing her head in the direction of the ocean and handing him the beach bag.

Suddenly as they turned a corner at the end of a street, there was the ocean.

"Is that it?" He danced along.

"That's it."

"When can I put on my suit?"

She stopped at a hot dog stand and rented a blue umbrella, the biggest umbrella Tomás had ever seen.

There was nothing but sand between a row of houses and the water. People were scattered all along the beach, lying on blankets and towels, in the sun or in the shade of umbrellas. Children of all sizes were running, shouting, wading, digging.

Tomás followed Barbara, sinking into sand at every step.

"Can I take off my shoes?" he asked.

"In a minute." She led the way to an unoccupied place on the sand about halfway down to the water.

"How about setting our umbrella up here? The tide's coming in. If we go closer, it'll chase us back in no time."

He looked around at the people near them. Some had chairs and tables.

"Do they live here?"

"No. They've come to spend the day and want to be comfortable."

She opened the umbrella, so that it rested on the sand. "First, we'll make you a little dressing room." She took a big bathtowel from the top of the basket and draped it across one half of the open umbrella. "There, put your suit on in there."

He took the red trunks from the bag and pulled them on in a hurry.

"Do they fit?" she asked from the other side of the towel.

"I guess so." He strutted into the sun.

"They look fine," she said. "You did a good job of picking them out."

"I buy lots of things," he boasted. "Rice and bread and eggs and magazines and candles."

"Candles?"

"I only buy candles sometimes," he said, wishing he had not mentioned them, but she was busy working the umbrella pole deep into the sand.

"Where's your suit?" he asked.

"I'm wearing it." She unbuttoned her shirt and Tomás saw a yellow swim suit underneath.

She put the camera in the basket and covered it with a towel.

"Ready?" She held out her hand to Tomás.

Together they ran across the sand to where it dipped smooth, wet, and shiny down to the waves.

At the water's edge, he pulled back. Barbara let go of his hand, leaving him feeling both glad and sorry. Underfoot the wet, dark sand almost tickled, it felt so smooth and firm. Every place he stepped the water made a silvery footprint.

He watched a wave flow back into the sea, leaving a tiny white shell. He ran to pick it up, holding it for her to see.

"Look, a shell!"

The next instant the wave caught him, boiling coldly over his feet.

"Agh!" he shouted, leaping out of its way. And

suddenly Barbara was laughing at him. He began to laugh, too.

"It caught me!" he screeched, running down to the water's edge and giving it a kick. It turned and came back. He ran from it, shrieking.

Soon he became used to waves coming and going. He ran whooping and splashing, first along the edge, then dared to go deeper until the water foamed around his knees. Barbara watched him for a while, and then swam out beyond the breaking waves. He could see her yellow bathing cap bobbing beyond the green walls of water.

He poked along the water's edge, looking at bits of glass and pebbles made smooth by the sand and water. He noticed the different kinds and sizes of shells. He picked up the prettiest and the unbroken ones until both hands were full and he had to run back to the umbrella to dump them down beside the basket. He would take these as a present to Fernanda. He went back to gather more.

Barbara came riding in on a wave and waded out of the water, breathless and dripping.

Together they went back to the cool sand under the umbrella. She spread a striped towel for each of them. Lying on his stomach, face propped in his hands, Tomás watched a tiny girl shovel sand into a pink bucket. When the bucket was full, she carried it down to the water and dumped it in.

"How far down does the sand go?" he asked, worrying that perhaps careless children might carry it all away.

"I don't know." Barbara sounded puzzled. "I suppose it goes down a long way."

"Deeper than I could dig?" he asked, working his fingers into it.

"Oh, yes."

"Who put it here?"

"Who? Why, the ocean. The water grinds and grinds against big rocks for thousands of years. It wears them down to these minute particles that we call sand."

140

Barbara spread sunburn lotion over his face and back and gave him the bottle so that he could put it on his arms and legs and chest himself.

Far out he saw three small white boats.

"What are those boats doing out there?" he asked.

"Fishing," she said.

"Could you swim that far out?" Tomás asked.

"No," she said, "not half that far."

Tomás ran off to wade again, and, after that, they ate sandwiches and shared a banana and drank soda. Then Barbara made him lie in the shade and rest.

The wind felt exactly right. His skin felt dry and tight. He thought of Fernanda and sighed. If only she were here, everything would be perfect. I have to talk to the doctor, no matter how scared I am, he told himself.

And then he was asleep.

16

BACK TO MANHATTAN

When he awoke, Barbara was wearing black sunglasses and drawing on a pad propped on her knees. He reached out and patted her bare foot. The sunglasses turned toward him.

"Hi! Have a nice nap?" she asked.

He smiled and lay looking out at the sparkling sand and sea. He wished he could live here forever, except when it snowed.

He sat up.

"Would you drive your car to Puerto Rico?"

"Most of the way, yes. What made you think of that?"

"It's always warm in Puerto Rico. If you go, would you take me with you?" If she would take me, he thought, I can coax her to take Fernanda, too.

"Wouldn't your mother miss you?" The black sunglasses turned his way, then back to the child she was drawing.

"I don't have any mother."

"Oh? I didn't know that, Tomás." She stopped sketching to talk. "What about your father?"

Tomás shrugged. "He doesn't come home so often."

"You *live* with your aunt, then," she said. "You're *not* just visiting."

"It's a very long visit, and I think perhaps she is growing tired of me—of us—my sister and me."

"Is your sister the one who's afraid to go outside?"

"Yes. Fernanda."

"What about school?"

Tomás shrugged again and threw out his hands, shoulder high. "There are schools in Puerto Rico."

"How can Fernanda go to Puerto Rico if she's afraid to go outside?"

"Your brother could cure her!" Tomás had his plans all worked out. "Your brother could cure her, and I'll bring fish and vegetables to eat, so you can save money for gas, and I'll save some money, too, and when we have enough, we'll go."

"Well, that certainly sounds ingenious, Tomás."

"What's that mean?"

"Clever. Well thought out. But I'm afraid it's not that simple."

"Why not?" Grownups always made things hard.

"For one thing, it takes more money than we could save on just fish and vegetables. And we don't know if my brother can do anything to help Fernanda. But I'll speak to him and maybe he'll come to see her. And right now we have to start for home. What time are they expecting you?"

"They don't care," Tomás said.

Briskly, Barbara began to gather their things. "It'll be growing cool soon, and besides we have to get home before the rush hour traffic starts, though luckily most of it will be going the other way. Is your suit dry?"

Tomás felt it and nodded.

"You can put your clothes right on over it then," she said.

The ride back was long. The sun, also heading westward, shone right in Tomás's eyes.

When at last they crossed a bridge, Barbara said, "We're back in Manhattan."

Tomás felt glad.

They left the car at the garage and walked home. As they came to Barbara's building, they saw a man standing at the door. He had thick white hair and wore a light suit. He looked hot, but not cross.

"Charles!" Barbara cried.

He greeted her with a smile. "Hello, Barbie."

"How long have you been here?" she asked. "You should have called. I might have missed you!"

The man kissed her cheek and took the basket. "But you see, you didn't miss me," he said smiling. "I had to come downtown on business, so when I finished, I took a chance and came over. Do you know, it's five degrees cooler down here?"

Tomás stood there feeling left out. At last Barbara turned to him. "That's why we live here, isn't it, Tomás?" she said lightly. He felt her hand on his shoulder. "Tomás, this is my brother."

"How are you, Tomás?"

Tomás scowled. "Okay."

Barbara took the blue bag from Tomás's hands. " 'Bye, Tomás. I'll see you tomorrow," she said to him. She turned back to her brother. "Are you as thirsty as I am?" Tomás heard her ask as she unlocked the street door.

He did not hear what the doctor answered because they went inside, and the door slammed and locked itself behind them.

Too late Tomás remembered that the shells, seaweed, and pebbles for Fernanda were in the bottom of the blue bag.

Going up the stairs of the Pérez and Salvador tenement, Tomás decided to go and knock on Barbara's roof door and ask for the shells. Perhaps she would give him a cold drink, too. After all, she had promised to let him talk to the doctor, although now he didn't know whether he wanted to or not. He was probably all right, her brother, but Tomás hoped he wouldn't come visiting often.

Tomás reached Barbara's roof and made his way

across to the open skylight directly over the kitchen. Below, the refrigerator door slammed. An ice tray thudded in the sink. There was the sound of running water followed by ice cubes clinking into a bowl.

"Charles?" He heard Barbara call. "Charles, what about people who are afraid to go outside? Are they hard to cure?"

She was out of sight, but right below Tomás, at the table.

"Depends on the cause."

"What about a child?"

"How old?"

"Fourteen, I think."

Tomás leaned down close to the open skylight.

"All disturbances are easier to cure in children. Is it someone you know?" the doctor was saying.

"Yes. Tomás's sister, Fernanda."

There was a silence and then Barbara said, "It's the usual story, I guess. Tomás doesn't give out with much, but I gather the mother's dead, and the father doesn't often come home. They seem to live with an aunt. Today he asked if I'd take him to Puerto Rico with me. And his sister."

Her voice sounded amused.

The sound of her voice made a lump form in Tomás's throat and then go away when she added, "Maybe I will."

He heard quick footsteps, the doctor's, walking from

the living room rug across the bare floor to the kitchen. "You're not serious," he said.

"Yes, I am."

"Saddling yourself with two kids?"

"Why not?" Barbara asked.

"What for?" the doctor said. "Children are bad enough when they're your own, but somebody else's . . . ?"

Barbara's answer reached Tomás clearly. "I suppose you're right. You always are. Take your glass. Let's sit in the living room."

Tomás tiptoed away.

It's *his* fault, he thought, growing angry. She would have taken us to Puerto Rico. If it wasn't for *him! He* will never help Fernanda.

17

THE ACCIDENT

Reaching his own roof, Tomás walked more briskly. Fernanda would want to hear about the beach. She would expect him to be happy. If only he had the shells he'd collected. On impulse he stuck his hand in his pocket: sure enough, there were three. He took them out—one dark blue, one pink, one white shell—*and* a smooth white pebble.

He put them back in his pocket, pattered across the roof, and started down the iron ladder in his usual surefooted fashion. But, somehow, he stumbled. He lost his grip on the side of the ladder, fell and hit the landing, his weight all on one foot. As he crashed against the barred railing, his ankle turned.

Pain shot up his leg. He ground his teeth to keep from screaming. Tears sprang to his eyes.

Fernanda shrieked and came running to the window. "Tomás! *Qué pasa?* Ay! *Madre de Dios!*"

He rocked back and forth, gasping, unable to speak or think.

Fernanda tried to haul him inside, but he shook her off.

"Are you badly hurt?" she kept demanding.

"I don't know."

Slowly, slowly the pain eased. He dared not move his foot for fear the hurt would begin again. He wiped his eyes and his sweating face on his sleeve.

Gently he eased himself on his hands to the window and swung his legs through. Gingerly, he put his weight on the other leg and stood up. With Fernanda's help, with ouches and *ays,* he reached a chair.

Fernanda untied his shoe and propped his leg on a box. She had been drinking coffee. Quickly she mixed him a cupful.

Drinking it, he began to feel better. He reached in his pocket for the shells. They were unbroken.

"Look," he said, "aren't they pretty?"

By emptying his pocket he was also able to show her a handful of sand. "See, this is what the beach is made of. You can run in it and dig in it—and even pour it back into the water."

Now he looked at his ankle again. It was swelling. He was frightened. They soaked it in hot water, but it had no feeling, except of water burning his skin.

Against his will, Fernanda turned his foot this way and that until one unfortunate movement made him shriek and kick at her with his good foot.

"I'm sorry," she apologized. "I think it's broken."

152

"How can it be broken?" he scoffed. He believed that broken legs looked like broken tree limbs—bent and hanging.

"It will be all right tomorrow," he promised. "You'll see."

They ate supper and then Fernanda read from a book, asking Tomás to tell her the words she did not know. He fell asleep. Presently she woke him and helped him into bed.

In the middle of the night, his leg began to throb. Tomás moaned and rolled over. His foot and ankle continued to ache.

"Fernanda," he called. "Fernanda, my foot hurts."

He heard her moving, and felt her hands as she knelt beside him. "Could I have a drink of water?" he asked.

She brought him a glass of water and went back to bed, leaving him to doze and wake, and cry quietly to himself.

When he opened his eyes, the light in the room told him the sun was shining. Fernanda came in with coffee and bananas.

When he had eaten his breakfast, he limped out to sit in the kitchen. He watched Fernanda wash the dishes, then wash the clothes and hang them on a rope.

He wondered if Barbara would miss him. She had asked him to come that day for more posing. He had kept from thinking about her words, but now he heard the doctor's voice again: *Children are bad enough when they're your own, but somebody else's.* And her reply: *I suppose you're right. You always are.*

The pain in his chest seemed worse than the pain in his ankle.

When he made himself stop thinking of Barbara, he worried that Mrs. Salvador or Mrs. Pérez might send to Mrs. Malloy's building for him to baby-sit.

It did not occur to him that Barbara would be the one to hunt for him.

However, as that day passed and the next, Barbara grew worried. By the afternoon of the third day, she was saying to Omar, "I hope he didn't get sick from too much sun." She decided to go and find out.

In the downstairs hall of the tenement, she read the mailbox names. Lorca. No box bore that name, but of course his aunt's name might be Salvador or Pérez.

Mrs. Pérez opened the door of 5A. Young Fidel peered around her skirts.

"Good morning," Barbara said. "Is this where Tomás lives? I haven't seen him lately. I wondered if he was ill."

"No-o, he not live here," began Mrs. Pérez. "He live up the street. There is another apartment there."

"Up the street?" Barbara echoed.

"*Sí*. Two block. Up the street. This way." She pointed north.

Barbara frowned. "I thought he lived here with his aunt."

"No. Not here."

"Oh," Barbara said, puzzled. "Thank you very much."

"I not see him either, for two, three day, maybe. He baby-sit for you, too, eh?"

"No, I draw pictures of children, and sometimes he poses for me." Barbara thanked Mrs. Pérez and went back down the worn staircase.

She started north along Greenwich Street, wondering what apartment house Mrs. Pérez was talking about. Something was odd. She was very puzzled. If Tomás doesn't live in that building, how did he get locked out on the roof? she asked herself. Maybe, she thought, his aunt does not have a Spanish name, and he *does* live in the building.

Just then, however, she saw the curtained windows of Mrs. Malloy's building. This had to be the one Mrs. Pérez meant. It was the only apartment house in the block. She stepped into the hall. A small sign said SUPER, APT. 5.

She reached Number 5's door and knocked.

"Who is it?" a voice inside shouted.

Barbara raised her voice. "I'm looking for Tomás Lorca."

The door opened. Mrs. Malloy was wearing a large black-and-white apron over her dress, and holding a broom. Orange Clancy rubbed against the broom, purring.

"And what would you be wanting with him, Miss?" she demanded.

"I took him to the beach Tuesday," Barbara began. "I haven't seen him since, and I wondered if he was sick."

"Come in, come in!" Mrs. Malloy swept Clancy aside with the broom and stood at attention like a sentry. Barbara stepped into the shining kitchen.

"Have a chair, have a chair," Mrs. Malloy ordered. "Do you live in Brooklyn?"

"No. No, I live down the street," Barbara said, again puzzled.

Mrs. Malloy's blue eyes grew round. "You've seen Tomás around here?"

"Yes." Barbara nodded. "Doesn't he live here?"

"That he does not." Mrs. Malloy shoved the broom in the corner and sat down. "If that don't beat Pat! The little devil told me they was going to Brooklyn to visit their godmother, and off they went—clothes and all. That was weeks ago."

"He's visiting an aunt," Barbara explained. "Doesn't he have an aunt in this building?"

Mrs. Malloy shook her head. "Not him!"

Barbara raised her eyebrows. "I've seen him every day or so till this week. First he said he was visiting his aunt at the apartment building next to the butter-and-egg place. Later he said he lived with his aunt. The Puerto Rican woman in that building said he lives here. She sees him every day or so, too," Barbara added. "I believe he baby-sits for her."

"If that don't beat Pat!" Mrs. Malloy repeated.

"You mean he doesn't have an aunt at all?" Barbara asked.

"No! Maybe he ain't even got a godmother. Let me see now—" She got up and began rummaging through a drawer in the white cabinet spotted with red roses. "Where did I put that name and address? Got it here somewhere. Saw it the other day."

"I gather Tomás's father only comes home now and then," Barbara said.

"Not no more, he don't." Mrs. Malloy paused in her rummaging. "That poor man's gone from this world, if you ask me—may his soul rest in peace. I can feel it right here." She clutched her stomach. "Malloy says he's gone to Puerto Rico. But I tell him he's wrong. Mr. Lorca wouldn't've just up and left those children."

"But if something had happened to him, wouldn't someone have let you know?"

"Who?" Mrs. Malloy asked.

"The police—"

Mrs. Malloy gave an immense shrug.

"The question is," Barbara insisted, *"where is Tomás?* Could he be staying with some other family around here?"

Mrs. Malloy turned her head slowly left and then slowly right. "There used to be a Puerto Rican family around the corner, but they moved months ago. . . ."

Whenever Mrs. Malloy was upset, she put on the teakettle. She did it now. When it began its shrill whistle, she asked: "Would you like a nice hot cup of tea or coffee, maybe?"

Barbara said she would. She was getting a tight, frightened feeling. She told herself not to be silly. Of course *someone* knew where Tomás lived. Eleven-year-old boys did not live by themselves. *Someone* was looking after him.

But who?

18

WHERE THERE'S SMOKE

Barbara sipped coffee while Mrs. Malloy found the godmother's name, got the phone number from information, and dialed. The Mrs. Fernanda Ravello who answered had, of course, never heard of Tomás.

Barbara and Mrs. Malloy now began to be really worried. Mrs. Malloy said over and over again that Mr. Malloy was due home in a little while and that when he came, *he* would know what to do. Her faith made Barbara feel more cheerful.

Soon they heard Mr. Malloy's step in the hall, firm and confident. The door opened, and in he came, round and curly as ever. He looked hot and sweaty. His thick gray hair lay in damp ringlets around his forehead. Even his eyelashes curled.

"This is Miss Ransome," Mrs. Malloy said. "She lives down the street."

Mr. Malloy said, "Pleased to meet you," and shook hands.

159

"What a day!" he went on, dropping his cap and lunch pail on the nearest chair. "Anything cold?"

"Wait till you hear this!" Mrs. Malloy said, opening a can of soda and pouring it over a glass of ice cubes. Mr. Malloy drank it while they told him about Tomás.

"So the kid never went to Brooklyn, after all," he said. "So he's living around here somewhere. Gotta be!"

"But Fernanda," Mrs. Malloy cried. "What about Fernanda?"

"She's with him, of course. As sure as my name's Patrick A. Malloy."

"And what are they doing for food?" Mrs. Malloy demanded. "How could he take care of her? How can they be keeping clean? Lord love us, Malloy, and here all this time I've been thinkin' they was safe in Brooklyn!"

"Take it easy," Malloy said. "That kid's no dope. He'd get along. He found you—" He nodded at Barbara. "You said you paid him for taking his picture, didn't you? Selling fish from the fish market, running an errand or two."

"And baby-sittin'," Mrs. Malloy put in. "He told Miss Ransome he did baby-sittin'."

Malloy nodded again. "Maybe he took their clothes to the launderette once in a while. Between them they hardly own more than a good handful."

"But where is he now?" Barbara's fear grew. "Last time I saw him he asked me to take him to Puerto Rico with me if I went this winter. And he wanted me to find

160

out about helping his sister."

Malloy leaned both elbows on the table. "You thought he lived next door because he came by the roof, eh?"

He shook his head admiringly and clucked. "I'll tell you where he's hanging out—imp that he is. It's as plain as the nose on your face. He's hanging out in one of those empty buildings up this block or another. There's dozens of places where kids like them could sleep and never be noticed. Never be noticed at all. Leave it to Tomás! He's been looking after himself since he was three and done a good job of it. And he's smart in school. I've seen his report cards."

Mrs. Malloy's face beamed. "Now didn't I tell you himself would come up with the answer? He knows this neighborhood, Lord love him!"

"Lived here all my life," Malloy bragged. "Used to be all nice houses here—"

"But what if he's sick?" Barbara interrupted him.

Malloy thought that over. "That kid's never been sick a day in his life," he announced, "but I'll take a look around."

"You can come with me," he added graciously, "if rats don't scare you."

They scared her, but they would not stop her.

"Now don't you worry," Malloy told his wife. "We'll find them. Want I should bring the girl back here?"

"Of course bring her back here. Where else would you take her?"

He turned to Barbara. "Maybe you'll want to keep the boy till we decide what's to be done."

"Oh, yes," she said.

Meanwhile, Fernanda worried. Three days had gone by, and Tomás's ankle was now blue and swollen. Only a little food was left.

If I dared to cross the roof, she thought, I could go to Miss Barbara for help. Perhaps after dark I could . . .

She had an idea. Tomás had told her that Miss Barbara sometimes painted on the roof. If I build a fire, while it is still daylight, she thought—a small fire that would make a little smoke—Miss Barbara might see it and come.

She put a crumpled newspaper into the fireplace and lit it. She glanced at Tomás in the next room. He had not stirred.

The paper burned too fast to give off much smoke. She lit another and another. Suddenly smoke billowed into the room, making her cough.

Tomás awoke. "What are you doing?" he screeched. He jumped up, forgetting his ankle, and sank back with a groan. "Put that out!" he shouted. "Get some water!"

Fernanda hated to be shouted at. She stalked out and came back with a bucketful. She hoped Miss Barbara had seen the smoke by now. Angrily she splashed water into the fireplace.

Tomás lay back. "I'll be all right tomorrow," he

promised. But he was still in pain and no better than he had been yesterday or the day before.

As Barbara and Mr. Malloy started up the street they heard fire sirens. They paid no attention: engines went clanging past every day or so. By the time they had climbed to the roof of the apartment house where the Pérezes, the Salvadors and Bert lived, the shrieking trucks seemed to have come to a stop down below.

"Better see what's going on," Malloy said, and led the way to the parapet at the front of the roof. By standing on tiptoe, Barbara could lean far enough over it to look down. Two red and chrome trucks were drawn up in front of the building, engines running, red lights flashing. A third was screaming down the street to join them. Men in black helmets and black rubber coats swarmed in every direction, opening fire plugs, connecting hoses. Several who were carrying axes walked methodically across the sidewalk and into the building.

"They're coming in here," Malloy said, astonished. "There's no fire in this building. Guess we'd better wait a minute to see what's up."

Sure enough, they heard trampling on the stairs, and then a booted, black-coated fireman burst onto the roof. He took a quick look around and turned back to shout down the staircase. "Tell that woman to stay inside. The fire's not in her building."

163

Another fireman came up the stairs, breathing hard, and another and another.

"Where's the fire?" the first demanded, seeing Barbara and Malloy. He shoved his helmet back to wipe sweat from his forehead.

Malloy shook his head.

"You folks see any smoke?" demanded the second.

"Not a wisp," Malloy said.

At that moment the fireplace in the cave room chose to send up one last puff. The little cloud waved above the chimney like a flag.

"There!" A fireman pointed. He set off at a run, his rubber boots thumping across the tarred roof. The others followed.

"Smoke from a fireplace? That's a fire?" Malloy shouted.

"It's an empty building," one of the firemen shouted back at him as they bounded across the rooftops.

"That'll be Tomás," Mr. Malloy said to Barbara. "Come along."

"Should we?" Barbara held back, afraid of getting in the firemen's way.

Footsteps sounded on the stairs. A hand slapped the metal door and flung it open. Barbara took a deep breath and ran after Mr. Malloy.

Three of the firemen disappeared down Tomás's fire escape; a fourth ran to the front wall and waved his arms at the men still down in the street below.

Barbara followed Mr. Malloy down the ladder and

164

in through the apartment window. He gave her a hand as she jumped from sill to floor.

The firemen were running in and out of doors.

"Someone's living here," one man shouted, noticing how clean everything was and the drying clothes.

Malloy looked at Barbara. "What'd I tell you?"

Before she could answer, a fireman shouted, "You folks live here?"

"No," they both shouted back.

One of the firemen came stomping up the dark stairs. "I been clear through," he announced. "You men get to that room up front? That's where the fire is. No place else."

"The door's locked," they yelled.

"Break it down," he yelled back.

Barbara stood half-hidden behind Mr. Malloy's broad back in the hallway and hoped no rats would be frightened out of the building. More and more boots came climbing down the fire-escape ladder outside the window.

Suddenly the light from a powerful flashlight filled the room.

"Stand back and give him room to swing," the fire chief ordered.

The ax glinted in the light, and the wood of the door splintered. At the second blow, the door burst open.

"Anybody in there?" A beam of light cut the darkness.

"Kids!"

"Two kids!"

"Hey, what is this? What're you kids doing here?"

At that moment, for one instant as the light hit them, Barbara saw two pairs of enormous black eyes in two small, pale faces—Tomás and Fernanda, huddled under a blanket.

166

A fireman pushed past Barbara with an air of authority.

She saw by his white helmet that he was the chief. The Market watchman was behind him, and behind the watchman was a policeman whose broad shoulders further blocked Barbara's view of Tomás and Fernanda.

"You turn in the alarm?" the chief was asking.

"I did," the watchman said.

The chief reached the room. "These kids start the fire? Okay. Get 'em out of here."

"That's him!" the watchman cried. "I knew when I saw the smoke." He rushed at Tomás and hauled him roughly to his feet. Tomás screamed as pain shot through his ankle.

With a roar Malloy plunged forward like a football tackle.

"Keep your hands off those kids!" he yelled.

"Bit me!" the watchman yelled back. "He bit me!"

The men all began shouting at once. No one seemed to see Tomás who was rocking back and forth on the floor moaning, "My foot, my foot!"

Fernanda's shrill voice cut through the din, "Eeee-yiiii . . ." she yelled. "His ankle. It is broken, you pigs and dogs! If you hurt him, I will kill you all!"

Barbara hoped no one else understood Spanish.

There was a dead silence for a few seconds and when the men stopped milling around, Barbara saw that Mr.

167

Malloy was carrying Tomás into the daylight of the kitchen. Fernanda ran along at his elbow.

"I can say in my report that you'll take care of this?" the chief was asking the police officer as the last pair of firemen's boots disappeared up the ladder.

"Yes, sir," the officer said, swinging his night stick nervously.

The chief nodded and went out the window and up the fire escape.

Malloy sat on one of the two chairs and held Tomás on his lap. Fernanda stood at his shoulder.

The watchman looked at his bitten hand and was starting to tell the policeman for the third time how he'd suspected Tomás, when the policeman interrupted him and said, "All right, Ernie, go put something on that hand. I'll let you know if I need you."

The policeman turned his back on the watchman and bent to look at Tomás's swollen ankle. Tomás let the policeman move his foot this way and that.

"There might be a small bone broke," the policeman said.

"Que dice?" Fernanda demanded sharply.

Tomás told her in Spanish.

"Now—" The officer looked from Mr. Malloy to Barbara. "What is all this? Do these kids belong to you?"

Barbara began to explain, and the officer wrote some words in his notebook. He took Barbara's name and

168

address and telephone number. Then he took Mr. Malloy's name and address and telephone number. "They'll have to go to the station for now. Welfare will take over on Monday."

Fernanda shrank behind Mr. Malloy's broad back.

"This child needs a doctor," Barbara cried.

The policeman sighed. "Lady, we have doctors."

"But the girl needs a psychiatrist." Barbara did not give up. "She never goes outdoors. She'll be terrified."

"How you going to get her out?" Mr. Malloy demanded. "You try to haul her up that ladder against her will, you're liable to hurt her."

Barbara explained about Fernanda. "My brother's a psychiatrist. He could treat her," she said finally.

The policeman looked at his wristwatch. "What do you want me to do? I can't leave them here. You want to take them home and give them a bath and be responsible for them until Monday, it's all right with me. But I gotta get them out of here."

Barbara and Mr. Malloy were quick to accept the responsibility.

"Okay," the policeman said, "I'll go call an ambulance. One of you can go along to the hospital with the boy. I'll have the doctor give the girl a shot to keep her calm. She won't be any problem at all."

Tomás was glad to hear Barbara say that she would go with him to the hospital and that afterwards she would take him home to her apartment. Fernanda

169

would be taken straight to the Malloys, and when she woke up, she would find herself in familiar surroundings.

Tomás raised his chin and looked Barbara bravely in the eye. "Are you going to give us to Welfare?"

Barbara looked at Mr. Malloy. "I hope we can work out some other arrangement. Something they'd like better."

"We'll see," Malloy said, and Tomás had to be satisfied with that. It was Barbara and Mr. Malloy's turn to ask a few questions. They began by asking how he had hurt his ankle.

It seemed no time at all before there were footsteps on the roof again, and the policeman came back down the ladder with the doctor who was carrying a black bag.

The doctor jumped through the window, set his bag on the table, and opened it.

"This the girl?"

"Yes." The policeman put one arm around Fernanda's shoulder. Miraculously, she did not fuss. "Come over here by the window, honey," the policeman said. "The doctor wants to see your arm."

"What's that?" Tomás gasped, catching sight of a shiny glass tube and the point of a needle. The doctor held it up to the light.

Mr. Malloy's big hand closed over Tomás's mouth. "Shhh," Malloy said in his ear. "He won't hurt her."

The doctor dabbed Fernanda's arm with a piece of cotton. With a flick of his wrist he slid the bright needle under her skin before she knew what was happening or had time to see what he held.

Tomás saw her jump, but she made no sound. The next instant the needle was out, the arm swabbed again with the cotton, and the doctor was walking back to his bag.

"There. That didn't hurt, did it?" the policeman asked, letting go of Fernanda who flung herself across the room toward Tomás and Mr. Malloy, but Barbara caught her and held her close.

"*Cálmate, cálmate,*" she said soothingly. "You're all right now. Pretty soon you're going to feel sleepy, and then we'll take you home to Mrs. Malloy."

19

A VISIT FROM WELFARE

Tomás was not allowed to stay until Fernanda grew sleepy. The doctor looked at Tomás's ankle, nodded, and said, "The ambulance is waiting. Let's go."

Malloy handed Tomás out the fire escape to the policeman, and with no trouble at all the policeman carried him up the ladder, across the roofs, and down the stairs. Tomás wished Bert, Mrs. Pérez or Mrs. Salvador could see him being carried off by a big policeman, but they met no one.

Barbara followed and climbed into the back of the ambulance to sit on a little seat near him. The policeman went back to Mr. Malloy and Fernanda.

The doctor came into the ambulance and sat beside the driver. They set off quietly.

"Isn't he going to blow the siren?" Tomás asked.

"I guess not," Barbara said. "You're not an emergency case."

But the siren did growl as they crossed Broadway. It didn't rise to its full shriek, but it did growl loud enough to stop traffic.

"Here we are," Barbara said.

At the hospital the driver lifted Tomás out of the ambulance and sat him in a wheelchair.

Tomás didn't know whether to be scared or whether to enjoy the ride down the corridor and into the examining room. Barbara was beside him all the way. After a while they wheeled him to the X-ray room where, Barbara explained, they were going to take pictures of the bones in his ankle.

While the X-rays were being developed and studied, a nurse wheeled him back to the examining room. There they sat and waited for a very long time.

"Do you think Fernanda is asleep by now?" Tomás asked, nearly asleep himself.

"I'm sure she is. I expect Mrs. Malloy has her all tucked in bed."

Barbara went out for a few minutes and came back with hamburgers. At last the doctor came. He reported that Tomás had no broken bones, but he did have a bad sprain. He took a big roll of bandage and wrapped it around and around Tomás's ankle and foot.

Tomás and Barbara went home by taxi, which was almost as exciting as the ambulance. The taxi man drove faster.

Barbara paid the driver to carry Tomás upstairs. When they opened the door, Omar barked crazily, as though to ask, "Where have you been all this time?" Owa the Siamese jumped down from the window sill

174

and came to sniff Tomás's bare toes which were sticking out of the bandage.

"We'll unwrap the bandage so you can take a bath and soak your ankle before bed," Barbara told him.

She filled the big white bathtub nearly to the top with water and after he had bathed himself and put on his shorts to sleep in, she re-wrapped the bandage. Then she put him in her bed and said she would sleep on one of the pink couches.

"Tomorrow we must get you a pair of pajamas so you can be a proper invalid," she said. "Now, how about some hot chocolate?"

She went into the kitchen and he heard her whistling while she fixed the hot chocolate for them both. Then she read to him until he fell asleep.

On Saturday morning Barbara telephoned her brother. Barbara told Tomás to call him Doctor Charles. He came in the afternoon, bringing red pajamas for Tomás.

Tomás scowled, but the red pajamas and Doctor Charles's friendly manners made it hard to stay mad at him. Girls being what they were, Tomás thought Fernanda would probably like the doctor a lot.

Doctor Charles asked Tomás how he felt, and then said, "Tell me a little about your sister. Do you know why she doesn't like to go outdoors?"

"Maybe because of my grandmama," Tomás began. And he told the doctor about their life until now.

The doctor asked a question once or twice, and finally he said he would go talk to Fernanda at the Malloys'.

"Is there any message you'd like to send her?" he asked. The question reminded Tomás of Sabertooth and McCall.

"The cats! Our things!" he said, thinking how Fernanda would be worrying about her scrapbooks.

"Your things will be all right for a couple of days," Barbara assured him. "And I'll take a can of cat food to McCall and Sabertooth in a few minutes. I'll also make sure they have water."

"Could Doctor Charles take Fernanda her scrapbooks?" Tomás asked. "And maybe an old magazine? She would probably be more friendly if you took them to her."

"I don't see why not," Doctor Charles said, smiling. "That's a good idea. I couldn't have thought of so good an introduction."

Barbara looked through a stack of magazines lying on the coffee table and handed three to her brother. A fourth she gave to Tomás in case he got tired of reading and wanted just to look at pictures.

Barbara and Doctor Charles left by the roof door. Tomás found it hard to concentrate on either the book or the magazine while Barbara was away. He coaxed Owa over to the bed and patted him as he listened for Barbara's footsteps.

When at last she came, she called out, "Everything's fine. The cats were curled up asleep, waiting for you, as though nothing had happened. We found the scrapbooks and your clothes. Charles took Fernanda's to her along with the scrapbooks, and I've got yours."

Tomás was relieved. They talked and Tomás told Barbara how he got food every day and how Fernanda had made a comfortable home for them. Then he lay back on the pillows and feel asleep. He was very tired.

When he woke up, he heard the doctor talking to

Barbara in low tones in the living room. He wished he knew what they were saying, especially about Fernanda and Welfare.

The rest of that day and all of Sunday, Barbara fixed Tomás's meals on a tray, gave him books to read, and fussed over him like a baby, but he did not enjoy it. He couldn't wait to be outside again.

Finally Barbara said, "Why don't you talk to Fernanda for a while? Here, I'll dial for you."

"Let me," Tomás begged, so she gave him Mrs. Malloy's number.

He heard it ring, and then Mrs. Malloy's voice on the other end. He began to giggle so much he could hardly talk.

"Lord love you, it's Tomás!" she cried at last. "Fernanda!" And then Fernanda's voice came shyly over the wire.

"Oh, Tomás," she said as she grew used to talking on a telephone, "Dr. Charles is so nice! In a few days he is going to take me to his hospital and help me not to be afraid. Then I will go in the street, and to school —everywhere!"

"I will walk over and see you before you go," Tomás promised. "Tomorrow, or the day after."

On Sunday evening, he got out of bed and limped around the room.

178

"Remember what they said at the hospital," Barbara warned him, " 'Stay off that foot for at least three days.' "

"I want to be able to walk when Welfare comes tomorrow," he explained.

"That won't be necessary," Barbara said. "I'm just going to have a talk with them. I'm pretty sure you'll be staying with me till your ankle gets well."

Tomás flopped back onto the bed. "Then I hope it *never* gets well."

Barbara smiled and smoothed her hair. "Yes, you do. How would you go to school?"

Tomás scowled at her. What did she know about Welfare? "You don't need to care whether I go to school or not." He turned his back to her. "You won't have to worry. You'll never see me or Fernanda again after Welfare gets us."

"Tomás!" Barbara dropped down to sit on the bed beside him. "Where'd you ever get that idea?"

He told her about Juan García, and what the kids at school said.

"That is just plain not true. And to show you how wrong they are, I'll tell *you* that Welfare is so interested in your being taken care of that they're willing to pay *money* for your food and clothing! Anyhow, you don't really know what became of Juan García's family. Maybe Welfare found them a nicer place to live—"

"This is a nice place to live," Tomás said.

179

"I know. But I mean out in the country—"

"Juan García liked it here."

"But maybe now he likes it better there. You just can't know. Besides, we're talking about you and Fernanda. What would you say to staying here with me while Fernanda goes to a hospital for a few months, until she learns not to be afraid out-of-doors?"

"Would I ever see her again?"

"Of course, Tomás! You could even visit her every week."

"Is this what Welfare is going to do?"

"In a way. My brother works as a doctor for the City part of the time, and he has talked to Welfare about Fernanda."

"And he'd cure her?"

"Yes. There is every reason to hope so, my brother says."

"And after that?" he asked. "Then can we both live with you?"

Barbara put her arm around him and hugged him tight. "I'm afraid not," she said gently.

"I know." Tomás was resigned. "You're going to Puerto Rico."

"Not only that, but Welfare thinks children need a father as well as a mother."

"Then why don't they find my father?"

"They're trying," Barbara said.

Tomás's heart felt suddenly lighter. "If Papa comes back, then we won't have to worry, will we?"

180

"You don't have to worry, anyway. The first thing is to get Fernanda well. After that, we'll take the next step." She rose and started toward the kitchen.

"Hey!" Tomás cried suddenly. "Hey, Barbara, would Welfare give me the money? If they would, I could buy another stove and fix that place all up with window-glass, and we could go back there and not bother anybody."

Barbara shook her head. "No, they wouldn't give it to you. It has to go to a grownup."

"They could give it to you—and you could give it to me."

Barbara laughed and shook her head again.

Tomás shrugged. Things went like that. He thought of the Malloys. "Would Welfare pay for Fernanda, too?"

"Yes, I think so."

"Then maybe the Malloys would take us both. Mr. Malloy is too old to have to worry about more mouths to feed." Tomás quoted Mrs. Malloy.

"There's still a question of where you'd sleep," Barbara said. "Welfare may not think the Malloys have enough room for you." She looked at her watch. "Okay, that's enough talk for tonight. Lie back now. I'll bring you a glass of milk."

Tomás awoke very early. He could tell how early it was by the gray light at the front windows. Omar lay stretched asleep at his feet. No sound came from Barbara and Owa up front.

He had been dreaming. What was it? A nice dream. He tried to remember. He had been back in their hideout, that was it, only it was all clean. The floors were still gray, bare boards, but the walls were white. He frowned, trying to remember. It was the hideout, but the rooms were different. In fact, it was like the apartments in Mrs. Malloy's building—like his old home, except reversed—at the *back* of the building. Like the empty apartment behind the Malloy's, that was it! Number Seven.

No one lived in Seven. Something had gone wrong with the plumbing years ago. From time to time when a pipe or fitting was needed elsewhere, Mr. Malloy took it from there. Mr. Malloy said the landlord did not want to spend the money to fix up the apartment.

Tomás sat bolt upright. The idea came bright as sunshine: If Welfare would pay the Malloys money for Fernanda's and his food and clothing, then he and Fernanda could each have a room in Apartment Seven! *And* their own living room so as not to bother Mr. Malloy when he came home tired and wanted to read the paper or watch TV.

He could see the whole thing clearly. Fernanda sitting at a table in the front room, a lamp shining on the book in front of her—not a scrapbook, but a schoolbook. He could even see the dress she was wearing, a plaid school dress. As though this were a doll's house with the roof cut away, he could see Mr.Malloy in front of the TV with his shoes off.

No, he was wrong. What he saw was himself and Fernanda, not studying but doing dishes in Mrs. Malloy's kitchen. Then Mrs. Malloy was plopping down in a chair near her husband. "Lord love those children!" she was saying. "They're as good as gold."

Maybe she wouldn't say just that, Tomás thought, coming back to reality, but she does like Fernanda, and I could run errands and do lots of things for her.

Impatient for Barbara to awake so he could tell her his idea, Tomás nudged Omar onto the floor with his good foot.

"Go get her," he whispered. But Omar yawned, stretched, and jumped back onto the foot of the bed.

He had to wait to tell Barbara until she was cooking breakfast.

"It sounds like a good plan," she said cautiously. "It's up to the Malloys, of course, but I can speak to them tonight—after we know what Welfare is going to say."

Welfare that morning turned out to be just one man wearing a brown suit. He introduced himself as Mr. Ross.

"Are you sure this is Welfare?" Tomás whispered to Barbara.

"Yes, I am. Why?"

"I thought they wore black uniforms with gold badges, and gold buttons, kind of like cops."

The talk with Mr. Ross took almost all morning. Barbara proposed to keep Tomás while Fernanda spent

183

a month or two in Doctor Charles's care. By that time, she hoped Welfare would be able to find out what had happened to Papa. They told Mr. Ross the whole story, beginning with the time when Papa had not come home. Then without warning Barbara said she was going to take Omar for a walk. Tomás was left alone with Welfare.

It was not so bad as he expected. In fact, it was not bad at all. Mr. Ross was nice. He just asked questions, like a teacher, and Tomás answered them all. Yes, he felt bad about Papa's being gone. He liked the idea of staying with Barbara. He did want to go back to school.

At last Barbara came in.

Mr. Ross said he was sure everything could be worked out as Barbara wanted it. He promised to come back in two days with papers to fill out.

20

REACH FOR THE MOON

One evening three months later, Tomás was again opening a door and stepping onto a roof. This time he had a right to be there: it was the roof of the Malloys' building.

In one hand he carried an old telescope that belonged to Mr. Malloy. He opened it up and steadied it against the chimney and trained it on the moon. He had to make a report on the moon at school tomorrow. But he had to hurry because Doctor Charles was bringing Fernanda at eight o'clock. That was when the party would start. It was all for Fernanda. At the Malloys. And Barbara was coming.

The morning after Tomás had told Barbara about his idea of living in Number Seven apartment, Barbara had talked it over with the Malloys.

"Bless my soul, did you ever see the like of him!" Mrs. Malloy had exclaimed. "Malloy, is there any reason under heaven why not!"

Tomás had watched Mr. Malloy, not breathing, just hoping.

Mr. Malloy was shaking his head, but there was a twinkle in his eye. He turned to Tomás. "When two women get their minds set," he said to him, "you might as well give in." He looked at his wife. "You got your heart set on raising 'em. Go ahead."

"Oh, boy!" Tomás ran to give Mrs. Malloy a quick hug, and she folded him in a hug so tight he had to wriggle free to breathe.

They talked about fixing the bathroom and painting the rooms, and Barbara offered to pay for it. Then she and Mrs. Malloy talked to Mr. Ross of Welfare and the landlord. A few days later Barbara reported to Tomás that the Malloys had been to the Welfare office and that Mr. Malloy had then gone uptown and talked to the landlord about breaking through the wall between the Malloys' apartment and Number Seven and making a door. The landlord was agreeable and set a very low rent for Apartment Seven. A week later Welfare advised the Malloys that the living arrangements had been approved.

That was more than three weeks ago now. What with school and helping get Number Seven painted and furnished, he had not had much time to visit Barbara. He was eager to tell her that Mr. Malloy said he worked better than the helper he had on the job.

And now Fernanda was coming home—home to the Malloys, to a real bedroom of her own, and a living room to be shared with Tomás. It was all just as he had

186

dreamed it might be that morning months ago at Barbara's.

Tomás and Mr. Malloy had painted and painted and painted, until now the rooms looked brand new. Their belongings from the other place were stored in the kitchen, waiting for Fernanda to decide where to put them. And Mr. Malloy had brought their beds, the TV, and the other furniture up from the basement. With his help, Tomás hung George Washington and the map in the living room. Mr. Ross paid them another visit and thought everything looked fine.

Mrs. Malloy said it would not be necessary for Tomás to get free vegetables and fish from the markets any more, so he promised to help her in other ways.

Now, Tomás thought, gazing through the telescope at the craters on the moon, everything is going to be wonderful if Fernanda is really cured and if only she will like going to school! Then he remembered Papa.

He turned the telescope from the moon to a star. Mrs. Malloy said Papa was up there somewhere, higher than the trails of jet smoke, higher than the satellites and the moon. Papa had not stopped coming home because he stopped loving them. He had been killed in a traffic accident. The police had found a card in his pocket. It had his name on it, but no address. And after many weeks the police finally traced him to Mrs. Malloy's.

Tomás had cried when Barbara told him. He remembered how she had dropped into a chair beside the table and held him close, and he had cried and cried until her shoulder was all wet. Afterwards, as she wiped his face with a washcloth, he had bragged, gulping, "I never cry."

"Me neither," she had said, and he saw that her eyes were red, too. Without being told, he knew she must like him a lot if seeing him cry made her cry, too.

Tomás picked up the telescope. He closed the roof door behind him, locked it, and started downstairs. He heard voices and laughter below. Then Fernanda came running up the last flight of stairs. Barbara and Doctor Charles were with her.

"Tomasito," she called, catching sight of him. "I'm here! I'm home!"

She was wearing a pink and white dress that he had never seen before. A pink band was holding back her hair. She looked beautiful, and almost grown up.

"I came all the way here in Doctor Charles's car, and I wasn't afraid. Not the least bit," she was saying breathlessly. She hugged and kissed him until he pulled back through the apartment door.

She gasped to see the new white walls. Sabertooth came out of the bedroom, stretching and yawning.

"How big he is!" Fernanda cried.

"Look!" Tomás was calling. "Here's your desk, and your lamp, and over here—here's mine. And come in here—"

188

Doctor Charles and Barbara followed them from room to room, with Tomás proudly acting as guide. The Malloys brought up the rear. Everyone talked at once, shouting to make themselves heard. Then they all trooped into the Malloys' living room to have the ice cream and cake.

To make the occasion even more festive, there was a present for Barbara. Fernanda had finished the apron, and wrapped it neatly.

"It is for you," she said, laying it in Barbara's lap. It was beautiful. The ruffle was exactly right, and when Barbara put the apron on, the strings tied in a crisp bow. Tomás nearly burst with pride. All evening, too, he had been noticing how easily Fernanda spoke English.

At last Doctor Charles and Barbara rose to go.

"Omar will be wild with delight when he finds you're going to walk him every day," Barbara said, referring to the new job she had offered Tomás.

"Fernanda can come visit you, too, can't she?" he asked.

Doctor Charles smiled at her. "She certainly can."

Barbara and he said goodnight and went downstairs, and then Fernanda and Tomás said goodnight to the Malloys and went through the new door into their own living room. Sabertooth ran to them, and Tomás scooped him up and handed him to Fernanda.

"Isn't it nice?" Tomás said to Sabertooth who was

190

purring in Fernanda's arms. "When you lived with us before did you ever dream we would have such a place?"

Fernanda looked around the living room. "Oh, it's beautiful, Tomás, just beautiful!" she said.

"It was nice before, too," Tomás said, loyal to the hideout, "but I think everything is going to keep getting nicer all the time."

After Fernanda had gone to bed, Tomás settled himself at the table that held his new lamp and his schoolbooks. He picked up his composition. Now he knew how to end it.

"Once people said you were crazy if you reached for the moon," he wrote. "But some men did it anyway. If you do not try, you never get to the moon or anywhere."